To my readers who fell in love with Maple Glen… Welcome back

CHAPTER ONE

Walking into Fran's Coffee every morning was something she would never get tired of. The city life was nothing in comparison to Fran's Coffee, the warm, inviting atmosphere a person felt once they walked through the wooden screen door and into Fran's.

September was the perfect time of the year for pumpkin spice and nutmeg *everything*. Fall seemed to last forever in Maple Glen, but Autumn wouldn't complain. In fact, it could last year round and she would be more than fine with it.

"Good mornin', sunshine," Fran called out from behind the counter. The woman never failed to greet her customers, no matter how busy she was. "You're just in time."

Autumn glanced in the direction Fran nodded. Their booth was packed. Emmalee, Clayton's girlfriend, along with Cara and a face she didn't recognize, were laughing over coffee.

Smiling back at Fran, she said, "Perfect, thank you!"

Walking toward the booth, she tried to figure out who the new girl was in the group. She had met just about everyone in Maple Glen—small town that it was—and couldn't recall the mention of someone joining their morning girl talk over coffee.

"Hey, Autumn," Cara called out, waving her over quickly. "I want you to meet Rylee."

Autumn held out her hand as Cara slid out of the way and Rylee stood from her spot. "It's nice to finally meet you," Autumn said, finally putting two and two together. They'd talked several times over the phone, but until now Rylee hadn't been able to make it to a face-to-face meeting.

"Likewise," Rylee said, her blue eyes shining in the morning sun squeezing through the blinds next to their booth.

"Cayden and Rylee made it to town late last night," Cara explained, and Rylee pointed to her skin underneath her eyes. "I didn't sleep much, if you can't tell from the bags I'm wearin'," she said, laughing as she held up her coffee. "I'll need plenty of *this* until I get used to the time zone."

"No worries," Autumn said, waving it off like it wasn't uncommon. It had taken her a few days to adjust. Sure, feeling tired all the time wasn't pleasant, but it hadn't lasted long. "I could've passed as an extra in a zombie movie when I first moved here from Minnesota."

The others laughed before sitting back down in their spots. Autumn couldn't help but think they'd need a bigger booth before too long—especially if they invited more girls to join them for coffee.

"Cayden swears I don't look *too* bad, but I made sure he knew that it's time for him to get his eyes checked," Rylee said, chuckling and taking a drink from her cup. "I mean, I appreciate him being so kind and all, but come on... I could definitely pass for the bride of Frankenstein for Pete's sake."

Cara nearly spit her coffee out of her mouth, hurrying to put her cup down and grabbing a handful of napkins to cover up the leaks. "That's freaking hilarious! But, seriously, you don't look *that* bad."

Rylee shook her head and silently rolled her eyes in disagreement. "Now you sound just like your brother."

Cara shrugged and said, "Maybe it's a Mitchell thing?"

"Definitely is," Emmalee chimed in. "Clayton tells me a hundred times a day that I look good. No matter how crappy I think I look, it doesn't matter."

Autumn couldn't help feeling a pang of envy as the girls shared their stories about the loves of their lives. She was happy for them, but at the same time, she would give anything to have that kind of happiness to brag about, too.

"So, tell me," Rylee said, looking across the table at Autumn with a friendly smile. "Is there anyone in Maple Glen that has caught your eye yet?"

Autumn's eyes widened. She had only just met Rylee. Well, technically, they'd talked over the phone for the last couple of weeks, but that had been strictly business. Nothing personal except when she asked for Rylee's dress size.

"Sorry," Rylee said, hiding behind her coffee before saying, "I shouldn't have asked—"

Autumn smiled, shaking her head and said, "No, it's fine. This *is* girl talk, right? That's what we're here to talk about, isn't it?"

Cara reached over and gave her hand a squeeze before looking at Rylee and saying, "Autumn has her eyes on someone alright, but he's a bit *too*... what would you say he is, Autumn?"

Autumn shook her head with a quick shrug. She didn't want to discuss Cara's brother right now. There were a million other things she could think of to talk about, and Charlie wasn't one of them.

"Ahh, the suspense is killing me," Rylee said. She

glanced at Emmalee and asked, "Do you know who it is? Am I the only one who doesn't know?"

For just arriving in Maple Glen, and this being her first girl talk over coffee with them, Rylee was fitting right in. Maybe just a bit *too* well. "Shh," Autumn said, pressing a finger to her lips. "Don't let Fran hear—"

"Hear what?" Fran said, moseying her way toward the booth.

Autumn eyed Cara and the other two, silently begging them to keep their mouths shut. "Nothing," she said, a bit too quickly, which made it obvious she was hiding something from the *Matchmaking Queen* of Maple Glen. She'd heard stories about Fran, and she knew better than to put the woman's abilities to the test. "We were just talking about Rylee and Cayden's wedding."

Fran slowly nodded, giving her a knowing look. *Busted.* "I see," she said. Then turning her attention to Rylee, she asked, "When's the big day?"

"October tenth," Rylee said, an ear-to-ear smile on her face. "It's actually the anniversary of when we first met."

"Isn't that just the sweetest," Fran said, making room to sit next to Emmalee before sliding in. "To be honest, I didn't know Cayden had it in him."

Cara laughed, and Autumn couldn't help but think about another Mitchell and wonder if he had it in him, too, or if he just couldn't care less about the whole *L* word. "You girls better get busy plannin', then," Fran said, interrupting Autumn's thoughts. "Time flies when you're havin' fun, ya know?"

Rylee smiled at Fran and said, "We're on it."

Another round of shared laughter, a few more drinks of coffee, and they were on to the next topic. "How are you likin' the bed and breakfast?" Fran asked, scooting out of her spot and stretching beside the booth.

"Actually, we like it," Rylee said, a dreamy look on her face as her thoughts trailed. "A lot."

"That's good to hear," Fran said. Turning to look at Cara, she said, "Last I heard, Catie was plannin' to fix it up here soon?"

Autumn sat silent as Fran and Cara discussed Catie's plans with the bed and breakfast. She hadn't been here long enough to know much about the happenings and goings-on around town. Which was mostly because she liked to stay to herself and focus on her business. She'd never been one to follow along with the latest gossip or the town's events, especially since she had spent the majority of her life living in the city. In the city, no one had time to talk about anything other than the weather and how jammed the traffic had been on the way to work.

She sure didn't miss living in Minneapolis.

"Anyway, I better get back to work," Fran said, rapping her knuckles on the table before turning to leave them to their own conversation. "I've got a newbie comin' in here soon, and he'll be learnin' the ropes around here. I wouldn't want him to catch me slackin'."

The girls laughed as they watched Fran make her way back to the counter. She grabbed the coffee pot and headed back to their table. "I figured I'd give y'all a refill. I wouldn't want you to continue coffee talk without the coffee."

"Thanks, Fran," they said in unison.

Emmalee's phone vibrated against the tabletop, causing it to do a little jig before she grabbed it. Swiping the screen, she answered the call and waved as she headed out the door.

"Must be Clayton," Cara said, watching as Emmalee

walked past the wide-open window in front of the coffee shop. "He must be missing her. He's such a big baby."

Autumn had met Clayton not long after moving to town with Cara. They'd made it a point to eat lunch at the deli so she could get a taste of Maple Glen and all that it offered. The smoked ham sandwich she'd eaten had become her favorite aside from tacos.

"When do you think he'll pop the question?" Rylee asked, once again fitting right in with the rest of them and wondering who'd be next. Autumn couldn't wait for her turn, but then again, she didn't want a turn if she couldn't have who she wanted. "We should place bets on it."

Cara laughed as she reached for her coffee, and Autumn nodded along. It sounded fun. Heck, at the rate things were going, Clayton could pop the question anytime—maybe even tomorrow.

"Grab a piece of paper," Rylee said, excitedly pointing at Autumn's planner. "Let's do this."

Autumn flipped to the back of her planner and grabbed a pen from her bag. "Okay," she said, scribbling their names down. "Rylee, what's your guess?"

Autumn glanced up at her, waiting for her to come up with an answer as she tapped a finger against her chin. "Hmm… they've been together for… what?" She looked to Cara for the answer, but quickly shrugged it off and said, "Oh, it doesn't matter. My guess is two weeks and a day from today."

Autumn couldn't help quirking a brow in her direction. "What?" Rylee asked, looking between Cara and Autumn. "I don't think that's too soon, do you?"

Cara shrugged and shook her head. Taking a quick drink of coffee, she set the cup back down in front of her and said, "I'll say…"

Autumn tapped the pen against the paper and studied Cara. Of course her best friend had to think about it forever before coming up with something. "Any day now, Care."

"Sorry, I just know my brother, and I think it'll happen at Cayden and Ry's wedding," she said, almost too matter-of-fact with a wide smile on her face.

Rylee's jaw dropped. "You really think he'd do that?"

Cara offered another shrug, and Autumn knew what she was thinking. There was no way to know for sure, but the chances were high, and it was a definite possibility. Autumn immediately started thinking of the perfect proposal.

She wouldn't want it to happen at another couple's wedding, that's for sure, but to each their own.

"Okay, so October tenth," Autumn said, scribbling the date next to Cara's name.

"Now you," Rylee said, grabbing the pen and paper, preparing to write down Autumn's guess. The trouble was, Autumn didn't know Clayton *that* well. She would more than likely lose the bet on that fact alone. But, not wanting to spoil the fun, she said, "I say by the end of this weekend."

"This weekend?" Rylee asked. Once again her jaw dropped open, and she looked at Cara like Autumn was crazy for saying it out loud. "Are you thinking, like, Saturday or Sunday?"

Autumn thought about it for a minute before saying, "Saturday night."

"How much are we allowed to bet?" Rylee asked, handing the paper and pen back to Autumn.

"Let's keep it simple," Cara said, reaching into her pocket and tossing a five-dollar bill in the center of the table. "Deal?"

"Deal," Rylee said, matching Cara's money with her own. Autumn followed suit and laughed. Fifteen dollars wasn't a lot of money, but then again, anything was better than nothing. That money could buy her a lot of coffee or a few ham sandwiches.

Cara smiled and nodded, snapping her fingers. "That's it."

"What?" Rylee and Autumn asked in unison.

"Autumn's going to win," Cara said matter-of-factly.

"Why's that?" Rylee asked, raising a brow in Autumn's direction, who offered a subtle shrug. Aside from just taking a wild guess, Autumn had no idea when it would happen.

"This weekend is the town's fall festival."

"Wait, what? Why haven't I heard anything about it?" Rylee asked, looking to Cara for answers.

Cara shrugged. "Maybe because you've got your mind on other things instead?"

"True, but still," Rylee said, tipping back her coffee and finishing it off before heading to the counter for a refill.

Autumn leaned forward onto her elbows and asked, "Do you really think Clayton will ask Emmalee this weekend?"

Cara offered a subtle shrug with a hint of a smile. "I don't know, but I'll make sure to keep my camera close by just in case. I'm all about catching the *Kodak* moments."

"Perfect!" Autumn said, wondering what she had planned for the weekend and coming up short after glancing down at her planner. Aside from weddings, her life was a snooze fest. Thanks to Cara, every once in awhile when she wasn't busy with Vince, they would go shopping and spend the day together, eating ice cream cones and talking about how great life was.

Rylee came back to the table, sliding in across from Autumn and Cara. Autumn opened her planner and grabbed a pen, preparing to jot down some much-needed information regarding Rylee's wedding plans.

"Okay, so before we run out of time," Autumn said,

clearing her throat. "Have you thought about what colors you would like to have in your wedding?"

Rylee looked from Autumn to Cara and back to Autumn. Autumn had seen the same look more times than she cared to admit. Most brides-to-be were clueless when it came to actually getting things ready for their wedding and choosing things, like wedding colors, for instance.

"Is it horrible to admit that I have no idea?" Rylee asked, panic crossing her face as she waited for them to answer her. "I guess I've put it off for so long, thinkin' I still had time to figure it all out, but now—"

"I told you," Cara said, letting Rylee know just how she felt but patting her hand to lessen the sting. "But it's okay. You have us now."

"Thankfully," Rylee mumbled, breathing a sigh of relief as she glanced over at Autumn. "Have you done a lot of weddings at the last minute before?"

Autumn couldn't help but laugh. Cayden and Rylee's wedding was far from being at the last minute. Sure, it probably felt that way to Rylee at the moment, what with everything piling up and her realizing there was still so much to figure out and to get done… but as far as last minute? Not even close.

"I've planned quite a few, actually," Autumn said, offering a smile before taking a drink of her coffee. If she was going to get anywhere with this wedding, she would need a constant flow of coffee. Rylee, thankfully, was nicer than the last bride she worked with on such short notice, so at least that was on her side, along with some extra time. "And we have plenty of time to plan yours. We just need to get busy with the tiny details so I can focus on the larger, more time-sensitive ones."

Rylee nodded and grabbed her phone, typing something on her keypad. "Okay, got it."

Rylee flipped her phone in their direction, showing them that she made a note to choose the colors. "I'll search through some images later with Cayden and see if he'll help me pick some out. I'm sure together we can narrow it down to a few and get back to you guys tomorrow?"

"Sounds good," Autumn said, jotting a note in her planner to meet Rylee again tomorrow. "What time?"

Rylee glanced between Cara and Autumn and shrugged. "I don't know. I'm fine with whatever you guys decide."

"How about—"

"Actually, can we meet at the same time we did this morning?" Rylee asked, taking a drink of her coffee and holding it up. "I kind of like this whole *coffee time with the girls* thing you guys have goin' on here."

"Perfect," Autumn said, marking down eight a.m. in the planner next to the little note she'd jotted down just a minute ago. "Gotcha down."

Rylee looked down at her phone, sent a message to someone, and slid out from her side of the booth. "Well, it's been fun, girls, but I've gotta run. See you tomorrow, then?"

Autumn and Cara nodded, then held up their coffee cups and said, "Yep," at the same time.

Rylee smiled and said goodbye, making sure to wave to Fran on her way out the door. Autumn was more than happy that Rylee was friendly and easy to get along with. It would make planning her wedding that much easier.

She didn't have time or the patience for bridezillas. And hopefully, since moving to Maple Glen, they were a thing of the past. So far, so good. Things were finally falling into place for their business, and planning a Mitchell wedding would be twice the fun. She just couldn't wait to plan Cara's.

The thought of planning her best friend's wedding had crossed her mind several times throughout the years of their friendship. And once Cara met Vince, there was no doubt she would have a future wedding to plan.

She couldn't help wondering if Cara thought the same about her. If Cara wondered if Autumn would ever find *the one* and fall head over heels in love.

Autumn silently chuckled at the thought of finding a love like those in the Hallmark movies, knowing the chances of its existence were slim to none. Especially here in a small town.

"Do you want to grab lunch after a bit?" Cara asked, pulling Autumn out of her distracting thoughts. "I'm going to help Fran clean up and head to my next photog appointment, but if you want, I'm all about grabbing some food afterward."

"Sure, that sounds great."

Autumn gathered her things, stacking them in a neat pile before shoving them inside her bag. She would head back to her place and look over her notes from the previous weddings in order to get an idea for what she wanted to do for Cayden and Rylee's. She also had a list of venues and catering services to look into before tomorrow morning.

Waving goodbye to Cara and Fran, she walked out the door and headed in the direction of her apartment. The same apartment that she had once shared with Cara. But it had become hers shortly after moving to town because Vince asked Cara to move in with him—a question they hadn't thought he would've asked in place of another, more *expected* question for two lovebirds wanting to spend the rest of their lives together.

CHAPTER TWO

Charlie had seen Autumn here and there around town but hadn't said more than a few words to her other than a few text messages when she'd first arrived in Maple Glen. Not that he didn't want to talk to her out in public, it was just the fact she always seemed too busy and didn't have time to sit for a minute.

He often caught himself wondering what she was up to lately, though ever since moving to Maple Glen with his sister, it seemed they were complete strangers. He had made it a point to text her when she'd first moved to town, but the texts slowly died down to nonexistent, and he wasn't one to chase after girls. If they didn't show interest, then he wasn't going to waste his time.

Today however, he'd had a slight change of mind about it and asked her to join him tonight.

"What are you thinkin' about, bro?" Cayden asked, hollering from across the bar. His kid brother had been there all afternoon tossing darts, shooting the crap with him, and not once made it a point to call him out on getting lost in his own thoughts.

Pushing away from the counter, Charlie straightened with a stretch. "Nothin' much, just wonderin' when you're goin' to take a break from throwin' those," he said, pointing to his brother's hand full of darts before glancing at the board. "I hate to break it to ya, but you kinda suck."

Cayden scoffed, flicking his wrist one last time while keeping his eyes focused on Charlie and groaning when the dart bounced off the side of the board and back at him. "I'd like to see you do any better."

Tipping his head back, he let out a loud laugh and walked around the counter. "Let me see 'em," he said, holding out an open hand and waiting for his brother to give him the darts. "I think you might've forgotten I *own* this place. Do you know how many late nights I've had to myself with this board?"

It was Cayden's turn to laugh as he grabbed a beer from the cooler. "Too many to count?"

"Maybe for you," Charlie said, jabbing his brother in the arm with an elbow. "Since you can't count past, what?"

That earned him a slight punch to the shoulder, but he shook it off. "Sounds like a pretty crappy life you've got goin' on if you spend most of your time alone playin' darts."

Charlie shrugged. He could think of a few things he'd rather spend his time doing, but that would involve finding a group of guys to hang out with and a good fishing spot. He knew Vince, Cara's boyfriend and Maple Glen's deputy, liked to fish at the ledge, but other than the few times they'd talked at family gatherings, he didn't know the guy all that well.

"It pays off," Charlie said, tossing a dart and nailing the bullseye. Catching sight of Cayden's jaw as it dropped from the corner of his eye, he tossed another dart, this time landing right outside the sweet spot. "For times like now when my brother challenges me to show him up."

Cayden shook his head and tossed back his drink. "Whatever you say, old man," he said, keeping up with the banter the only way he knew how—taking jabs about his age. Not that Charlie was *that* much older than Cayden, but whatever.

"Watch it now," Charlie said, flicking his wrist one last time while looking back at his brother, impressed when the dart landed in the center ring of the board. Not quite a bullseye, but he'd take it. "I may be older than you, but I've still got it."

"Dude, I don't even wanna know," Cayden said, feigning disgust as he shook his head.

"Get your mind outta the gutter, ya perv," Charlie said, nudging his brother. "That's not what I meant, and you know it. You should be ashamed of yourself for thinkin' like that. If Mom caught wind of that—"

"I'm a grown man now," Cayden said confidently, a smug grin on his face. "There's not much she can do about it."

Charlie shook his head and laughed. How naïve his little brother could be sometimes. "Mom brought us into this world, she can take us out anytime she pleases."

Cayden tipped his head back and let out a deep laugh. "There's no doubt you're right about that one."

Charlie stepped up to the board and removed the darts. Walking back toward Cayden, he extended his hand, offering his brother a solid shake. "Good game, brother."

Cayden reacted with a smug grin and asked, "How 'bout we play one more round?"

Charlie glanced at the clock on the wall. He didn't have anywhere to be until about seven, but he needed to leave himself plenty of time to get ready for his impromptu night out with Autumn. As long as she said yes. He was still waiting for her to reply back to the message he'd sent earlier.

"Why do you keep lookin' at the clock? You got a hot

date tonight or somethin'?" Cayden joked, offering Charlie a nudge in the arm.

"What if I do?" Charlie asked, his lips pressed in a thin line.

His brother took a second to read his expression but must have come up short because he asked, "Do ya?"

Charlie shrugged and stepped up to the line in front of the dart board. "I might."

Cayden slid onto a nearby barstool, silently waiting for Charlie to spill. Charlie laughed, and with another flick of his wrist he sent a dart spiraling straight toward the bullseye.

"Who in their right mind would want to date you?"

Charlie wondered the same darn thing. He wasn't much for love and all that mushy stuff. Heck, he even tried to come off as an ass most of the time in order to stay off women's radars.

But that didn't seem to stop a petite and pretty brunette from finding him. He blamed it on his sister. If Cara hadn't brought the city girl to town with her, he'd still be in the clear.

"What do you mean who would want to date me?" Charlie asked, straightening his posture and appearing confident in his physique. "Who wouldn't want to?"

Cayden laughed and tossed his darts one right after the other. Each hit the board, but nowhere close to Charlie's.

"Besides, you've got no room to talk," Charlie said. Stepping up to the line, he called out over his shoulder, "I still can't figure out why someone like Rylee would want to marry a guy like you."

Cayden gripped at his chest, stumbling back as though he'd been hit. "Man down. Man down."

"Cut it out," Charlie said, chuckling at his brother's antics. "You know I'm right."

Cayden's grin told him that he agreed. "I admit that a little bit of luck might be to thank when it comes to her."

Charlie tossed a dart at the board. "I'd say more than a little, but whatever."

"Anyway, let's talk about you for a minute," Cayden said, successfully changing the subject. "Who are you seein' tonight?"

Charlie contemplated telling his brother, quickly weighing the consequences before biting his tongue and shaking his head. Deciding not to tell Cayden, or any of his siblings for that matter, would be a smart move on his part. At least until he knew what was happening between him and Autumn.

"Come on," Cayden pleaded, but he wasn't going to get anything out of Charlie. "Fine," Cayden said, sliding off the stool and grabbing another beer from behind the counter. "I'll just take a few wild guesses."

"You can guess all day long. I still won't tell you," Charlie stated, keeping an eye on his brother as he walked toward him. He laid the darts on the counter and grabbed a nearby stool to sit on.

"What's the big deal? Are you afraid your family's gonna ruin your chances with her?" Cayden jabbed a playful elbow into Charlie's arm as he pulled up a seat next to him. Charlie wasn't afraid of his family ruining anything. He was more concerned with ruining it on his own. "Has Mom met her yet?"

"What?" Charlie asked, snapping back into the conversation. "No, no one has met her yet. Well, except..."

Cayden brought his beer to his lips, tipping back a quick gulp before setting the bottle back down in front of him. "Except who?"

Charlie shook his head. *Dang.* His brother was going to find out whether or not he wanted him to. "No one. Let's talk about your bachelor party. Are you plannin' on havin' one?"

"I guess so," Cayden said. "I don't know. Depends on whether y'all get your butts in gear or not."

Charlie knew it was up to him and his brothers to set something up. He wasn't good at planning things, but he had a rough idea of how his little brother's bachelor party should go. He made a mental note to get with the others before waiting too much longer. If they waited too long to get the ball rolling, they'd run out of time and his brother wouldn't have one before standing at the altar.

"Yeah, I guess that would help, huh?"

"Maybe just a little," Cayden joked, tipping back the last of his beer and placing the empty bottle on the counter. "Alright, I suppose since you aren't tellin' me anything, I'll head home and ask Rylee if she's heard anything at the coffee shop. I'm sure whatever is stirrin' up around town gets talked about in that little coffee chat the ladies have every mornin'."

Charlie nodded, knowing there was a good chance that someone would mention something. It hadn't taken long for the town to start talking the last time she was in town and they'd hit it off. Sure, it had only been one night—and there'd been nothing more than talking and sharing a few laughs between them—but it hadn't taken long for the town to catch wind of it and wonder what was going on between the two of them. "I guess you'll have to let me know. Seems this town always knows more about me than I do."

Cayden clapped a hand on Charlie's back and slid off the stool. "Nothin' new there. That's the small-town life for ya."

Charlie nodded, offering a quick handshake before seeing his brother out the door. He wondered if there was talk about him and Autumn, and whether or not it was a good thing. He didn't want to hide the fact that he was interested in her because she really was a sweet woman. And if he were to be honest, it wouldn't hurt for him to have something sweet in his life for a change.

CHAPTER THREE

Seeing the last minute text from Charlie asking her to hang out with him later sent her spiraling out of control with nerves, and she might have hyperventilated, too, if Cara hadn't been sitting across from her at the coffee shop.

She read the message again. This time, she studied it as she thought about what it implied. Was Charlie asking her on a date? At seven tonight. *No way.*

Unable to contain her excitement, but also needing someone to calm her down and help her gain control once again, she waved her phone at Cara. "He just asked me to hang out with him tonight."

Cara glanced up from her notebook and asked, "Who?"

Autumn couldn't believe she would ask such a dumb question. So much for the old-time saying *there's no such thing as a stupid question*. "Charlie. You know... your brother..."

"Like a *date*?"

Autumn looked back at the message and shrugged. "I'm not really sure. Maybe?"

Cara grabbed Autumn's phone and asked, "What do you mean you're not sure?"

Autumn silently waited for her best friend to read the messages from Charlie. "Well, it could just mean to hang out as friends."

Cara slid the phone across the table and nodded knowingly, even though she knew the two of them hadn't crossed the line separating them from being friends and something more.

"What am I going to wear?" Autumn asked. Panic consumed her voice and left her squeaky and a bit too high pitched. She definitely felt like a teenager experiencing her first crush. *Get it together*. She couldn't help but feel the rush as butterflies took flight. For being close to thirty, she shouldn't be as giddy as she currently was.

"Look at you," Cara said, pointing a finger in her direction. Autumn furrowed her brow. The last thing she wanted was for Fran—the resident matchmaker—to overhear and make a big deal out of nothing. "You're blushing."

Autumn fanned her face. "Of course I am. Now stop before Fran hears you."

Cara zipped her lips and tossed the key over her shoulder.

"Thank you," Autumn said, glancing toward the counter and making sure the coast was clear of any eavesdroppers. Looking back at Cara, she said, "Now help me decide what I'm going to wear."

"Well, that's not difficult," Cara said, tapping her finger against her notebook, and Autumn could almost see the thought bubbles before they burst. "Something casual, but sexy."

"Sexy?" Autumn didn't own anything *sexy*. It'd been years since she'd owned a closet full of club-worthy outfits, and once she started her own business, those went out the door, along with her spontaneity.

"Don't tell me—"

"That I've tossed nearly every *sexy* thing I've ever owned?"

Cara quirked a brow. "Did you?"

Autumn's cheeks reddened under the scrutiny of her best friend. Of course, the two of them were too focused on the contents of Autumn's closet to pay mind to Fran's location.

"This doesn't sound like plannin' a wedding to me," Fran said, motioning for Cara to scooch over as she slid in beside her. She glanced from Cara to Autumn, waiting for someone to give her the scoop, but neither one said a word. "Okay, then, if I had to take a wild guess, *this*," she said, motioning between the two of them, "has somethin' to do with Autumn's new love interest, *but* there's a chance I could be wrong."

Autumn's eyes widened as she stared at Cara, who was enjoying her aunt's intrusion in their conversation. Of course, Cara would be getting a kick out of it.

Fran leaned back, crossing her arms over her chest as she stared at Autumn, once again waiting for her to say something—whether to confirm or deny the fact that she was onto something. Autumn refused to give her the satisfaction of being right.

Cara took a drink of her coffee, trying her best to keep from spilling it along with the details of their conversation, but snorted in laughter while shooting coffee out of her mouth.

"Cara Lynn!" Autumn shouted, grabbing a handful of napkins and dabbing her planner dry. It was no use. The planner was spotted in large drops of coffee.

"I'm sorry… it's just… I can't—"

"Zip it?" Autumn asked, shooting a steely glare at her best friend. "That's quite obvious."

Cara reached over with a few napkins and helped clean up the mess she'd made. Autumn couldn't not forgive her friend. "Sorry, Care, I didn't mean that. I just—"

"You girls need a refill?" Fran asked, pulling herself out of an awkward situation. "I'll be right back."

Autumn watched Fran walk off. She wondered what the woman would say when she found out about Autumn's interest in Charlie. It wasn't like they were a *thing*, and she didn't even know if he liked her like *that*, anyway. The so-called date wasn't an actual *date* even though he did ask her to join him at the bowling alley, where a bunch of people were getting together for a few hours. The thought made her nervous. She didn't know anyone, and the only person she'd know…

"Why don't you want her to know?"

Cara's question interrupted Autumn's thoughts and pulled her back to reality.

She shrugged, not sure of how to answer the question. Maybe it was the chance of looking dumb or naïve if Charlie didn't like her the way she liked him. Maybe it was the fact she was scared to find out the truth.

"Well, you know she's going to find out sooner or later, right?"

Autumn nodded, knowing Fran's matchmaking ways would eventually find a way into her life.

But what if he wasn't interested in her the same way she was him? The possibility of embarrassment was higher if more people knew, including Fran.

It was bad enough she was his sister's best friend. Wasn't there a bro-code rule about not dating their sister's friends?

CHAPTER FOUR

He once thought he was a fairly patient man, but waiting on Autumn's response to his text message had proven otherwise.

Thankfully, she'd texted him back shortly after Cayden left the bar. It saved him from answering another round of twenty questions from his nosey brother.

Taking a deep breath, he grabbed his phone and read the message.

Of course! What time?

He read her message for a third time. She accepted his friendly invitation for her to join him at his bowling league tonight.

The invite *was* in fact just a friend asking another friend to hang out. Guys could be friends with girls, right?

Chuckling, he knew better than to believe the lies he'd been telling himself since she moved to Maple Glen.

He could pass the invite off as a *friend* thing about as well as he could look directly at her and not want to kiss those plum-colored lips of hers.

Shaking off the thought, he needed to keep it together. He

was acting like a teenage boy all over again, and that was the last thing he wanted. His parents raised him better than that. He was a gentleman, and no matter how attractive a woman was, he wasn't about to lose his manners.

Bowling starts at 7. Want me to pick you up at 630?

Dots bounced along the bottom of his screen as he waited for her to confirm. He wondered if six thirty was too early, or maybe it was too late. He wasn't good at this kind of stuff. Sure, he'd been on a few dates, but those didn't count because he only had one thing on his mind back then.

He was a different man now. Autumn wasn't like those girls he'd dated over the years. Aside from being his sister's best friend, he knew that she was sweet and down to earth. She was the type of girl every guy sets out to bring home to meet their parents.

Sure, I'll be ready. Finishing up the last bit of planning for the day.

He smiled as he read her text. He knew when Cara left town for the first time all those years ago, she was on her way to achieving goals and landing her dream job. What he hadn't known was that she would find a best friend and the two of them would work together in a wedding planning business.

He was about to text her and ask for her address when another message popped onto his screen.

Cara's old apartment ;)

Smiling because she had somehow read his mind, he replied with a quick **Got it** and shoved his phone in his pocket.

If he was lucky, he could play this off as *just friends* and keep himself in check. He didn't know much about her other than what they'd talked about that one night all those months ago, and even then their conversation didn't go super deep.

They'd been messaging each other for quite some time,

and never once had he invited her to tag along. But whatever had gotten into him today, making him invite her to his bowling league of all things, made him question his own motives.

Shaking his head, he pulled a bottle of water from the fridge and twisted off the cap. He chugged it and tossed the empty bottle into the garbage before grabbing another.

What kind of guy invites a girl to a bowling alley? The thought made him laugh. She was going to see the nerdy side of him, and he wasn't sure if that was good or bad.

Shrugging a shoulder after tossing the second empty bottle into the trash, he figured it was better to ask her to join him at the bowling alley than to a movie and dinner.

At least for now, until he figured out what it was he truly wanted in his life. So far, he was content with running his own bar and having time on the weekends to hang with the guys while fishing and tossing back a few cold ones.

The thought of losing that freedom made him question whether dating would be worth it. No matter how pretty and perfect the woman was, would she be worth losing the freedom to do as he pleased?

Grabbing his keys off a nearby hook, he headed out to his car. He wouldn't think about anything just yet. They were strictly in the friend zone for right now, and if he had a choice in the matter, he wouldn't cross that fine line between friends and something more anytime soon.

Parking in an empty spot in front of the apartment complex, Charlie shifted the car into park and killed the engine.

Before he had a chance to make it to the door, Autumn met him outside wearing a casual but attention grabbing outfit that consisted of a burnt orange tank top showing him glimpses of bare skin partially covered by a faded denim jacket. The rest of her outfit consisted of fitted dark blue jeans and boots. With her wavy brown hair softly covering her shoulders, along with the jewelry she decided to wear, she looked like she'd walked straight out of one of those magazines he'd seen his sisters occasionally thumbing through.

"Hey, you," she said, meeting him on the sidewalk.

"Hey," he said, swallowing down the lump forming in his throat as he tried to hide the effect she had on him. "I... um... hope you're ready for a good time tonight."

"Bowling?" she asked, a smile pulling at her lips. "I can't think of anything I'd rather spend my night doing."

He couldn't tell if she was being sarcastic or sincere. In the short time he'd known her, he'd caught onto the fact she was often sarcastic, but not in a demeaning way. She was actually quite funny.

"It works out that you agreed to come along tonight, because one of our guys in the league can't make it," he explained, watching her eyes widen in shock. "Are you good at bowling?"

"Wait," she said, holding up a hand to stop him from saying anything more. "Did you say league? Like, professional—"

"Not professional," he said, stopping her mid sentence, "but we're pretty good."

"I guess I should maybe go change?" Her question was more a statement than anything. "I might be a bit overdressed."

He didn't know fashion. Heck, he didn't know what city life was like, but looking at her now, he didn't have the heart to tell her she might be right. But, then again, she looked fine, and as long as she was comfortable, that's all that mattered to him.

"You know what? Let's just go," she said, motioning him toward the car. "I'll take some of this off on the way there."

He couldn't help but give her a questioning glance. One that silently asked *take what off?*

She laughed with heated cheeks as she slid into his passenger seat without waiting for him to at least open the door like a gentleman would have.

"You men... with your minds in the gutter twenty-four seven," she said, flipping the visor down and pulling out her earrings and taking off her necklace along with her bracelets. He was about to comment, letting her know that she was wrong. His mind wasn't in the gutter *all* the time. But before he could get a single word out, she flipped the visor up and said, "There. Now I'm ready for some bowling."

He nodded, agreeing that she'd toned her look down a notch and wouldn't stand out like a sore thumb among dorks who loved to bowl in their free time.

Shifting the car in reverse, he said, "Alright, let's do this, Ralph."

"Ralph?" she asked, quirking a brow at him as he guided the car in the direction of tonight's fun and games.

"Yeah," he said, allowing a smile to tease her a bit before saying, "you know, Ralph from *The Honeymooners*?"

She tossed her head back against the seat and laughed before looking back at him. "You think?"

Her laughter was contagious. He laughed along with her. "What? I'm just sayin'."

"Saying what? That I'm Ralph?"

He shrugged, inviting a playful slap to his arm. "Well, then that makes you Ed, Ed."

It was his turn to laugh now. "I'm more than okay with that."

She crossed her arms over her chest and jutted her bottom lip out in a fake pout. "Of course you would be. Why can't I be Barney from *The Flintstones* instead?"

He thought about it for a minute before he said, "That would make me Fred, and I'm not a Fred. An Ed, yeah, but not a Fred."

She slowly nodded, and he could tell she was thinking of a smart comeback, but after a minute she gave up with a sigh.

"Besides, I can't see you as a Barney."

He laughed, offering her a sly wink with a smug grin. She hated his banter, but he was enjoying himself. There was no crossing the line if they bantered like good friends, right?

"So, you never answered my question," he said, bringing her attention back to him. "Are you good at bowling?"

She offered a subtle shrug and said, "Maybe? It's been forever since I've actually played."

"Really?" For some reason, he had a hard time believing that. What did she even do for fun in the city? Not that he would ask that out loud, but he had no choice but to wonder what the city life was actually like if bowling and other fun wasn't a part of it.

"Yeah, I guess," she said, her mood dimming slightly, and he wondered what that was all about. Within a minute, she smiled and said, "Anyway, I can't promise I'll get strikes, and I sure can't promise I won't land a few balls in the gutter."

Laughing along with her, he was okay with that. He was far from a master at bowling. At the end of the day, it was all about the fun of the game and getting out of the house—doing something different every now and then.

"What's your highest score?" he asked, curiosity getting the best of him. He didn't care if she placed last tonight in points, as long as she had fun and enjoyed her time with him. *As a friend.* He shook his head. The whole friend-thing was going to be hard at the rate he was going.

She offered a small smile and asked, "Honestly?"

"Yeah, why not?"

"I think it was something like forty-two, or somewhere around there," she said, scrunching her nose. "Is that bad?"

He hid his chuckle as he said, "No, not *that* bad. I've seen worse."

"Ok, then it's bad," she said, shaking her head with a laugh. "I guess we'll have to see how horrible I am tonight, huh?"

"I guess so," he said, offering her a smile that he hoped would make her realize it wasn't a big deal.

Guiding the car into the parking lot, and dodging a few potholes larger than his car, he pulled into a vacant spot near the door and shifted into park.

Before cutting the engine, he looked over at her and offered her another smile before saying, "For what it's worth, I'm pretty sure there's a few on the league who will score way worse than you ever could."

Getting a smile out of her and seeing the dimples on either side of her face, he killed the engine and said, "Let's go and see what kind of damage we can do on the scoreboard tonight."

"Sounds good to me, Ed," she said, giggling like a school girl as she climbed out of his car.

"Okay, Ralph," he said as he watched her round the front of his car as she approached the driver's side.

Grabbing his keys from the ignition, he shoved them into his pocket and followed her inside. In just the short time they'd been together tonight, Charlie realized it was going to be a challenge to keep the *just friends* façade going without wanting something more.

Autumn was everything he'd want in a woman to give his heart to. A woman he'd want to spend the rest of his life with.

Shaking away the thoughts and blaming them on his brother's wedding and all the mushy vibes hanging around, he stepped inside and prepared himself for the questioning glances he'd get for bringing her along tonight.

Just friends. He needed to remind himself that no matter what happened tonight, they were *just friends*.

CHAPTER FIVE

Ten minutes in, and the so-called *date* wasn't anything she'd had in mind. It was apparent from the conversation in the car to the way he talked to her in front of his buddies, he saw her as *just* a friend.

She tried not to let it bother her, but she couldn't help it. The text messages they'd shared, along with the night of laughter and conversation that had lasted for hours, had obviously given her the wrong impression.

Abort. Abort. The word flashed bright in her mind. When she would normally send a message to Cara, begging her to help her out of a sticky situation, she couldn't tonight. Not when it involved Cara's brother.

"Hey, you're up," Charlie said, heading her way seconds after banking a perfect score. "Did you see that?" he asked, hooking his thumb over his shoulder in the direction of the lane. "Got a strike on the first roll."

Feigning a smile, she stood and wiped her hands on her jeans. If there was one thing that was going right tonight, it was the fact that she looked super cute in the multicolored and faded bowling shoes. "That's great," she said, expressing interest in order to not draw attention to her annoyance. Curbing her sarcasm, she gave him a high five as she walked past him. If he wanted to be just friends, then that's what he'd get.

"Strike 'em dead, girl!" One of Charlie's teammates called out as she grabbed a ball from the return. She smiled and said, "I'll try my best!"

Swinging her arm, she released the ball, giving it a whirl. Of course, the ball sailed straight into the gutter.

"Gutterball!" The guys hollered behind her, and she had no choice but to laugh about it. She never promised she was any good at bowling. Heck, she had admitted to Charlie that it had been forever since she last played. She didn't do much of anything other than shopping and girl talk over coffee.

Grabbing her ball from the return, she walked back to her lane and toed the line. This time, she focused on what she was doing, instead of on the one guy who distracted her the most.

After releasing the ball, she watched as it once again slid into the gutter. Tossing her arms out to her side, she spun too quickly and lost her footing.

Strong arms wrapped around her and kept her from falling on her backside in front of everyone.

He stared down at her with a smile on his face. It was more of a shit-eating grin, but whatever. She didn't care. He'd just saved her from humiliation.

"Thank you," she whispered, biting her bottom lip while trying to hide her embarrassment.

"You should take it slow and easy on these floors with those shoes on," he said with a wink as he kept an arm pressed against her lower back.

"Thanks for the heads up," she said, allowing her sarcasm to shine through. "You're a little late, though."

Dropping his arm and causing her to feel the loss of whatever kind of magic had transpired from his subtle touch, he said, "Sorry 'bout that. I'll try better next time."

Next time? She wasn't sure there'd be a next time. Sure, being his friend was great and all, but...

"You are comin' next week, right?" he asked, oblivious to the uncertainty of there actually being a next time.

"Am I?" Her question came out snarky, and if she could take it back, she would have in a heartbeat. She didn't want to give him the impression she was mad about something. That would lead him to ask a million questions, and it would only make things awkward between them. She'd done great so far with playing it off like she was enjoying her time out with him. *Maybe a bit too well.*

He took a step back, giving her space, and she realized she may have been a bit too harsh with her tone. Maybe she shouldn't have been so snarky. He looked down at the floor and back up at her. "I just..." he said, glancing over his shoulder before continuing, "I thought you were havin' fun?"

Feeling bad for being rude, she corrected the situation the best way she knew how to—by faking it. "Of course, I am," she said, waving a hand to dismiss his concerns. "I just thought this was a one-time thing is all."

"One-time thing?" he asked, quirking his brow with a slow nod. "Is that what *you're* wanting this to be?"

She was so confused. More confused than she had been a few minutes or even an hour ago. While his actions said one thing, his words were saying the complete opposite. What did Charlie Mitchell want?

"What is *this*, exactly?" she asked, once again letting a little attitude slip.

"What do you mean? What is *this*?" he asked. Now it was his turn for the attitude. "I thought it would be fun to invite you to come along for some fun. I thought you would enjoy it, but apparently I might've been wrong?"

"No," she said, wanting to stop the argument before it turned into something completely blown out of proportion. She knew she should have kept her mouth shut. "I had a lot of fun tonight. Actually, this is the most fun I've had in months."

"Then what's the problem?" he asked, crossing his arms over his chest. "I get the feelin' you're upset about somethin' and—"

"Look," she said, wanting to dismiss the argument while she avoided telling him how she truly felt. She had been wrong to think that there had been something transpiring between them. Especially over a few text messages. "It's fine. I'm fine. Can we just finish our game and leave?"

He gave her a look calling her bluff, knowing she wasn't fine, but he shrugged and motioned for her to walk past him. "Of course, if that's what you'd like to do, that's fine with me."

Walking back to the bench alongside the other teammates, she sat down and kept her eyes on everyone else while avoiding him. He sat down next to her, leaving only an inch of space between them. If she didn't know any better, she would assume he was trying to push her buttons. Make her crack and tell him whatever she had on her mind.

Giving him a side eye, she tried to keep herself from giving in. He caught her stealing glances and smiled. His dimples caught her attention, and she was done for.

"Can I help you?" His question was whispered as he stared straight ahead, not giving her a glimpse at his hazel eyes.

"Nope," she said, looking straight ahead and hiding a smile.

"Okay."

"Okay."

Lord help her, he was going to be the death of her if the game didn't end soon. She was over this night out. She was over the tiff they'd had. She was more than over thinking there was ever going to be anything more than just being a *bowling buddy* to him. Or, as he'd called her, *Ralph*.

Thankfully, the night out with Charlie had ended long before nine, leaving her a chance to relax while watching reruns of *I Love Lucy*. She'd blame her addiction to the show on her mother. Because of her, she had spent the majority of her teenage years binge watching late night television on *TV Land*.

Setting her phone down on the counter, she opened the freezer and reached for an unopened carton of ice cream. Before she had a chance to wrap her fingers around it, her phone vibrated noisily against the countertop. Debating whether or not to leave her phone unattended and continue on with her mission to indulge in her favorite cookie dough flavored ice cream, she leaned against the freezer and waited for the vibrating to stop. Only it didn't.

Sighing as she shut the freezer door, Autumn walked to the counter. Before grabbing it, she took a second to think. *What if it is Charlie? What should I say to him?*

Pushing aside her worries, she flipped her phone over and was relieved to see Cara's face smiling back at her. The picture was one they had taken together in a photo booth at the Mall of America. Swiping a thumb across the screen, she held the phone to her ear. "Hey, Care Bear," she answered, trying her best to sound casual and like everything was fine. "What's up?"

"I was about to text, but I figured I'd just call," Cara said, "How'd the date go?"

Autumn couldn't stop a burst of laughter. There was a chance that she sounded like a crazed lunatic, but she didn't care. Suppressing her laughter a bit, she said, "It wasn't a date."

She heard Cara tell Vince she'd be a minute and then the creak of a door. She must have walked onto the back porch. "Okay... now what'd you say?"

"Cara, it *wasn't* a date," Autumn repeated, knowing her best friend was having a hard time believing it.

"But—"

"I thought it was too... kind of," Autumn said, feeling the need to pull out the ice cream now more than ever. Swallowing her emotions with large bites of frozen chunks of cookie dough sounded really good.

"But?"

"But, he kept making references to being friends," Autumn explained, knowing it was as lame as it sounded. She had allowed herself the high hopes for nothing.

"References? What do you mean?"

Autumn wanted to crawl in a hole and escape with her reruns and a heaping bowl of ice cream. Instead, she stayed on the phone with Cara, who deserved an explanation because she *did* call to check in with Autumn. And because she was her best friend.

"I'm Ralph and he's Ed," Autumn said, sighing while praying Cara understood. She didn't want to break it down, or there was a chance she would cry. No, she wouldn't cry. She'd been through worse than having a crush and being kept in the friend zone. She needed to pull it together.

"Oh. My. God," Cara said, the words drawn out, "like in reference to *The Honeymooners*?"

"Yep, that'd be it," Autumn said, passing on the ice cream and heading straight for the bottle of wine she kept on hand for special occasions. This wasn't a special occasion in the traditional sense, but she couldn't care less as she pulled the bottle out of the fridge and popped the cork. "I guess it's not as bad as Fred and Barney?"

Slowly pouring the plum-colored wine into her glass, she heard Cara sigh. There was a minute of pause before Cara said, "Autumn, I'm so sorry."

She shrugged, as though Cara would be able to see through the phone. "Well, at least I know where I stand."

Carrying the glass in one hand, she held tightly to her phone with the other as she walked into her living room. The television was paused on the scene where Lucy and Ethel shoved chocolates into their mouths because the conveyor belt is running full speed and they could not keep up. Out of all the episodes, that one had to be her all time favorite.

"I'm going to have a talk with him," Cara said, interrupting the silence as Autumn drank her wine. "I hate to say it, but I don't believe it."

"Care, please don't," she pleaded. The last thing she needed was for Cara to talk to Charlie and make things more awkward than they already were. She'd left it alone once he dropped her off, and that's how she wanted it to stay. No need to stir up hard feelings or make him feel bad for not liking Autumn more than a friend would. "I just got carried away, is all. I read into something that wasn't really there. There's no need to force him into liking me."

Cara sighed, and Autumn knew what she was thinking. She didn't like staying quiet when things needed fixed. Cara reminded her of Fran in that way. The two of them shared similar traits, and Autumn could tell they were related. She could easily call them *Matchmaker One* and *Matchmaker Two*.

"It isn't forcing him to like you if he already does," Cara said, keeping her voice low.

"Care, we don't know that he truly does," Autumn said, silently pleading with her to leave well enough alone.

"You don't know my brother like I do," Cara said, and even though she hadn't meant the words to be a jab, they were. The words only echoed Autumn's realization from earlier that night.

"You're right," Autumn said, "I barely know him at all."

CHAPTER SIX

*P*ulling into an empty spot in front of his aunt's coffee shop, he shifted the truck into park and killed the engine.

He thought about what he would say if he saw Autumn inside, sitting at a booth with his sister. He knew they met at the coffee shop every morning for business relations, and he couldn't see why today would be any different.

The last thing he wanted was to make things awkward between them, but he couldn't help thinking it was too late for that.

Her mood had changed halfway through the game at the bowling alley, and she hadn't said more than a few words to him on the way back to her place while he was dropping her off. If that wasn't a sign he'd done something wrong, the fact she was ignoring his text messages was for sure.

He'd sent a text and was still waiting for a response. He'd thought about calling her, but he figured why bother someone who didn't want to be bothered.

Grabbing his keys from the ignition, he climbed out of his

truck and headed for the door. He needed a large coffee to go before he made his way to the Meat Locker.

The bell above the door chimed and announced his arrival, and the small tables were taken by several of the elderly residents who have lived in Maple Glen for decades.

His eyes scanned the rest of the area, landing on the booth toward the back of the coffee shop. Cara said something he couldn't quite hear, but he saw her lips moving—nothing unusual there. Out of all of his sister's, Cara was the most talkative.

"Well, well, well," Fran said, meeting him at the counter. "Look who we have here."

"Hey, Aunt Fran," he said, knowing it'd been a while since he'd last visited her. To be honest, he didn't get around to seeing too many of his family as often as he used to. After taking permanent ownership of the bar, along with competing against the one on the outskirts of town, he didn't have much time to focus on much else.

His mind flashed to Autumn, causing his eyes to find her sitting beside Cara. Her plum-colored lips formed a smile as she nodded to whatever Cara was saying. Betraying him, his eyes lingered for a second too long as they captured every detail about her.

"Ahem." Fran cleared her throat, pulling his attention back to the here and now. "Did you hear a single word I just said?"

Her question, though spoken with annoyance at his lack of paying attention, contained a dash of curiosity as she raised a brow.

He shook his head and offered an apology. She tsked him and asked, "Somethin' else got your attention? Or should I say, *someone*?"

He chuckled at his aunt's antics. Of course it was like her

to pick up on everything around here. There wasn't a single thing that went past her without being further inspected. And, with her playing the role as the town's matchmaker, she wouldn't have missed him studying Autumn. "I don't know what you're talkin' about."

Fran slowly nodded, offering him coffee in a mug instead of a Styrofoam to-go cup. "Would you be willin' to take this over to Cara for me, please?" she asked. "I hurt my knee while chasin' some pesky raccoons outta my trash cans last night."

He took the cup, wondering if what she said was true or not. It didn't matter. If it wasn't, he knew exactly what she was doing and he wasn't falling for it.

"Thank you, dear," she called out after him as he turned away from the counter and headed for Cara's booth.

Autumn's eyes caught his, and she quickly looked away. He was close enough to hear the mention of his bar, but everything else was a low mumble. He approached Cara's side just as Autumn mentioned frilly decorations and flowers.

"Hey, Char," Cara said, glancing up at him and down to the mug he was holding. "Are you joining us for coffee?"

His eyes betrayed him once again as they found Autumn's brown eyes staring straight at him—piercing through him. "I... uh..." he stammered, trying to find his words to explain why he was now standing there looking like a speechless idiot while holding a cup of coffee that was not his. "No, actually, Fran told me to bring this to you."

"To me?" she asked, jabbing a finger into her denim jacket. He nodded, but was surprised when his sister shook her head and leaned away. "That's not mine—"

"Fran said—"

A fit of laughter escaped Cara's mouth as she eyed Fran and looked back at him. "She got you."

Autumn bit her bottom lip and turned her attention away from him as she stirred a spoon in the caramel-colored coffee that matched her eyes. He wanted nothing more than to make the others leave so he could have a minute alone with her.

"Will you just take the coffee?" he asked, feeling humiliated and caught off guard.

"I don't drink black coffee. Otherwise I would," Cara said, pushing the mug away.

"Then why'd—"

"Because it was her way of getting you over here," Emmalee explained. He couldn't believe he fell for Fran's trick after telling himself there was no way he'd allow it. The trick was older than dirt, yet here he was, standing and looking like a complete idiot.

"Don't worry," Cara said with a laugh. "It happens to the best of us."

While the other girls laughed and made jokes, Autumn sat quietly as she avoided making eye contact with him and traced a finger along the rim of her cup.

The last time he checked his phone, she had yet to text him back and he was okay with it. But here she was, avoiding him completely except for a few subtle glances here and there. He would give anything to know what was going on inside that beautiful mind of hers.

"Do you drink your coffee plain?" he asked, knowing the question was random. And while his eyes were focused on Autumn, Emmalee answered with a scrunched face, "None of us drink it that way."

"Good to know," he said, taking the mug and turning to head back to the counter. But before he stepped away, he turned back and said, "The reception can be at my bar, but I'm not allowin' no frilly crap hangin' around."

Jaws dropped, but before any of the girls could say something about it, he turned back around and headed for the counter. Fran could take the mug of coffee and dump it down the drain for all he cared.

He should've been wiser than to fall for it, but whatever. Autumn didn't want him around anyway. She hadn't given him an ounce of her attention which pissed him off.

He set the cup down on the counter and was about to tell Fran just what his thoughts were on the whole situation when Autumn stepped up beside him.

"What do you mean *no frilly crap*?" Her eyes were filled with anger as she furrowed her brow and crossed her arms over her chest.

He chuckled. The city girl had an attitude, and she knew how to use it.

"What's so funny?" she asked, leaning against the counter and demanding him to answer as she stared him down. If looks could kill…

"Nothin'," he answered, pleased with getting the reaction he was looking for. If she wanted to ignore him, he would give her a reason. Sure, it was childish, and if his mother caught wind of it, he'd be up a creek without a paddle. It was no way to treat a woman, he knew that, but there was nothing wrong with ruffling feathers every now and then.

"It didn't sound like *nothin'*," she mimicked him, slight accent and all. She was adorable when she was mad. "Tell me why you don't want decorations at your bar for a *wedding* reception."

He didn't have an answer for her. In all honesty, he really didn't mind having decorations. Heck, a reception wouldn't be a reception without them. But he wasn't going to tell her that. But, he needed to tell her something. Thinking fast, he said, "Who would want frilly decorations in a manly place?"

"Well, obviously not sexist pigs like you," she said in a

huff before turning away and beelining it to the others who'd just witnessed the start of a war.

"Pig?" he asked, turning his attention to Fran who also saw the whole thing.

"She called you sexist, and the only thing you heard was *pig*?" Fran asked, eyeing him like he'd grown two heads and lost an arm in the process. "I'd rather be called a pig than be known as sexist, wouldn't you?"

He held up his hands, an attempt to call a truce. "I just came for coffee. I didn't ask for any of this."

"Well, it seems to me that you got more than you bargained for," Fran said, motioning over to Autumn's table. Autumn's mouth was moving a mile a minute—prattling on about him as she dug the daggers in deep, causing him to look away.

"Yeah, maybe so," he mumbled before saying, "Look, I don't need the coffee, anyway. I'll see ya later."

"Now you just wait a minute," Fran said, waving a hand in his direction to keep his attention. "I'll get your coffee, but you're going to tell me what's goin' on between you and *Plum Lips*."

He didn't have time to discuss it with Fran. He didn't even know what was going on between the two of them. Other then the fact he wanted her to text him back, which was neither here nor there. And then he wanted coffee. There wasn't anything else to explain.

Taking his coffee from Fran, he said a quick thanks before saying, "I'd love to stick around and chat, but Clayton's expectin' my help at the Locker today. Maybe we can chat tomorrow?"

He winked, and from the look on his aunt's face, he knew he was in trouble. For one, she hated when people, especially family, took their coffee and ran. And for two, he had started

World War Three right there in her coffee shop without an explanation.

He pulled the door open, allowing the bell to announce his departure before catching another dagger-filled glare from Autumn on his way out.

Wanting to be *just friends* seemed so difficult the day before, but now? It was a piece of cake, and he just managed to squash it.

~

"You did what?" Clayton asked, laughing as he stabbed his carving knife into the flank of yet another pig.

"I told them I wasn't allowin' frilly crap in my bar," Charlie said, knowing it had been as ridiculous as it sounded. More childish than anything, but then again, he had only wanted to get a rise out of her. It had been all in fun at first, but seeing her reaction…

"What the heck would you go and start that war for?" Clayton asked, splaying the left side of the pig open and carving out the salvageable meat. "I thought you were friends?"

"*Were* is the key word there," he said, knowing he'd messed up no sooner than the words had been spoken less than an hour ago. His phone had remained silent, even though he'd been hoping for something. Even an *I hate you* message would have been okay with him. But nope, nothing. If she wanted anything to do with him before his stunt, it was obvious that wasn't the case now.

"I don't know about you, man," Clayton said, shaking his head as he tossed a slab of pork into the smoker. "I thought you would have faced your fears by now."

Charlie took a step back. He wasn't sure what his brother

was talking about, but he sure wasn't ready to have a conversation about his weaknesses.

Clayton closed the lid of the smoker and turned to face Charlie. His brother knew better than to bring up the past, but unlike most of his brothers, Clayton also knew when to call him out.

"Do you like her?" Clayton asked, pulling off his gloves as he walked to the utility sink on the other side of the room.

Charlie stayed silent as he thought about how to answer his brother's question. Sure, he liked her. Whether that was something worth the headache he'd caused today, he wasn't sure.

"It's an easy question, bro," Clayton said, scrubbing his arms with soap and water as he stared at Charlie in the mirror above the sink. "It's a yes or a no. Easy as that. Quit overthinking and say it."

"Do I find her attractive?" Charlie questioned, buying some time to think of how he would answer the original question. He knew what it was his brother wanted to know. He wanted to know if Charlie liked her enough to date her and marry her. All of the Mitchell siblings were finding their happily ever afters, including Clayton, who had just found his happily ever after not too long ago when Emmalee had stumbled into town looking for her one of her own.

It was almost like he was living in a fairy tale made just for his family, but he was the only one not suitable enough for a happy ever after. *Go figure*. He half laughed at the thought.

"Do you?" Clayton questioned, bouncing the question right back at him and pulling him from his distracting thoughts.

"What kind of question is that?" Charlie asked, irritated that his brother was actually making him answer his own question.

"Just answer the question," Clayton said, drying his hands and tossing the rag in the trash. "You're makin' this too hard."

Charlie shook his head, pinching the bridge of his nose, and looked back at his brother. Of course he was making it hard. He didn't know easy. That was the story of his life. Everything he wanted involved an obstacle course—a challenge—and he had to overcome his own crap to get what he truly wanted.

Autumn would be no different.

"Yes."

His one word answer caused a smile on Clayton's face.

"But you're not attracted enough to make her your wife?" Clayton asked, arching a brow as he stood in front of Charlie. "Is that it?"

Charlie shook his head. *Of course not* was the answer he wanted to give, but he couldn't say it. Instead he said, "Wife? That's a bit drastic, isn't it?"

Charlie had a few years on Clayton, but that didn't mean much when it came to their conversations. Clayton was wise beyond his age. Heck, the guy had found his forever before Charlie had a chance.

"Not at all," Clayton said, grabbing a barstool and pulling it up next to Charlie before motioning for him to take a seat. Charlie accepted the offer, sat down, and waited for Clayton to tell him what he really wanted him to hear. He didn't have to wait longer than a minute before Clayton said, "I know you barely know her, but that doesn't mean a darn thing. Look at me with Emmalee. I knew the minute I met her, along with all of those crazy dogs she was walkin', that she was mine. There was just somethin' about the way I felt when she was around me—"

"Ah, cut it out already," Charlie said, laughing as he gave Clayton a light shove. "Enough with all of the mushy crap."

Clayton laughed, repositioned himself on the stool and said, "I'm not jokin'. If Autumn's *the one*, you'll know it. You'll want nothin' more than to spend every minute of every hour with her. She'll make all of your fears about fallin' in love disappear, and soon enough you'll be a man on your knees pleadin' for her to marry your sorry ass."

Charlie nodded while thinking of the night before. The night he'd spent with her at the bowling alley. It had been a short amount of time, but in the time he had spent with her, he knew Clayton was right about knowing when someone was *the one*.

CHAPTER SEVEN

"What was that all about?" Emmalee asked as soon as Charlie walked out the door and headed for his truck. Autumn watched as he climbed into the driver's side and backed out. *Good riddance.*

"Autumn." Emmalee's hand waved in front of Autumn's face, deflecting her attention from the guy who was no longer outside and was now her enemy. She no longer felt the connection she'd once felt with him. The spark that she had once felt between them was now a smoldering black cloud hanging between them. "What in the world just happened?"

"Was he joking?" Rylee asked, her question directed at Cara, who responded with a grimace and a subtle shrug as she mouthed an *I don't think so*.

"No, he wasn't joking," Autumn said, her tone sharp and full of anger. It upset her to think he could walk into the coffee shop and, without so much as a *hello*, tell her that the reception's venue—his bar—couldn't be decorated how she saw fit. Just because he hated frilly things? "And now we're without a place to host the reception after the wedding."

Cara stayed silent as she drank her coffee. It was apparent

she was thinking, so Autumn let her be. She wanted to drill her with questions. Ask her why her brother was so dang stubborn and why on earth he would do this. It was obvious he was only doing this out of spite. He wanted to get a rise out of her. *This* was the exact reason she chose business over relationships. She should have known better than to become attracted to someone who had no interest in her.

"I can't believe the nerve that man has," Autumn said, crossing her arms as she stared at her planner sprawled open in front of her. Her week was packed with planning opportunities, follow ups with potential clients, and making reservations. She needed to move reservations to the top of the list in order to make sure Rylee's wedding would have everything booked and ready for their big day. "Where are we going to have the reception now?"

Cara tapped a thumb along the edge of her mug, making it obvious to Autumn that she was still thinking. "He's doing it out of spite. I just know it."

"What would he do that for?" Emmalee asked, bringing her iced coffee to her lips and waiting for Autumn to answer while she took a drink.

"Because I didn't text him back," Autumn said, scrolling through their messages and silently cursing herself for not responding to him. Maybe if she would have taken a minute to let him know that all was okay, or that she really didn't care if he wanted to be friends, he wouldn't have acted out in such a childish manner.

"What? You're kidding, right?" Emmalee looked to Cara for confirmation that her brother could be so juvenile, but Cara only nodded with yet another shrug before she said, "Sounds like something he would do."

"Why are men so immature, anyway?" Emmalee asked,

before correcting with, "I mean, not *all* men, of course, because Clayton is well past that stage, thank God."

Autumn couldn't resist rolling her eyes. She obviously connected with the wrong brother. Check another tally off in the "fail" category. She didn't want to come off as jealous, because she was far from that. It was great that Emmalee found Clayton and fell madly in love. That would mean more business for Autumn and Cara in the future—the near future. Besides, she needed to focus on the things that mattered the most to her, anyway. Finding love had always taken the back burner in her life, and there was nothing different now. Just because she moved to a small town with her best friend, who had a single brother who was also a business owner and as handsome as the devil he was, didn't mean she was guaranteed to find the love she'd been missing out on for the past decade or so. "*Anyway,*" she said, focusing on what needed to be taken care of now instead of focusing on something she couldn't change. She had no control over that man's immaturity, and she wasn't going to waste time trying to change him. "We need to brainstorm some local venues who will have openings in October."

Emmalee slid out of the booth and said, "I've gotta run, but good luck. I know you'll figure it out. You and Cara are good at what you do."

Smiling, Autumn said, "Thank you. See you later."

Cara wrapped her arms around Emmalee and hugged her before allowing her to leave. "I'll call you tonight, and we can talk about Clayton and Vince's upcoming fishing trip."

A pang of envy shot through Autumn. She missed the late-night conversations she'd once had with Cara. The friendship they'd had for the last several years was taking a hit because of Cara's newfound love, and she could tell things were changing between them. Add one more thing to the mounting pile of things bound to fall apart.

"Don't worry about Charlie," Cara said, nudging Autumn as soon as she sat back down. "He'll come to his senses sooner or later and realize how big of a jerk he's being."

Autumn wasn't sure that was necessarily the truth, but it didn't matter. In the end, all that mattered was her business and making sure the Mitchell wedding she was hired for didn't flop. "It's okay," she said, trying to sound more confident than she felt. "I don't care what he says. We're having the reception at his bar, *and* there will be frilly decorations whether he likes them or not. It's not his wedding, and he's definitely not the wedding planner. I am."

"That's right," Rylee chimed in, taking a break from her never-ending conversation through text messages with Cayden—or at least that's who it appeared she was chatting with if her smile and giddiness were anything to go by.

Cara smiled and wrapped her arm around Autumn. "There she is," she said, snuggling closer in a hug, "welcome back, Autumn."

"What'd I miss?" Fran asked, sliding into the spot Emmalee had vacated not even five minutes ago. "How are ya doin'?" she asked, directing the question at Autumn. She smiled and said, "I'm good. He isn't going to rain on my parade."

"Thatta girl," Fran said, offering Autumn a fist bump from across the table. If there was an aunt Autumn would have wanted while growing up, it would have been Fran. She was laid back and easy going. There was no doubt she'd had her moments of stress, but now she was enjoying her time. "He'll come to his senses sooner or later."

"Then it'll be too late," Autumn said, trying once again to speak from a sense of confidence she wasn't sure existed when it came to Charlie, or any guy for that matter. "But anyway, enough about him. Let's focus on what matters, shall we?"

"We shall," Rylee said, placing her phone face down in front of her. Autumn wondered if Rylee had told Cayden what had transpired between his brother and Autumn. More than likely she had. Isn't that what people in relationships do? They told each other everything, didn't they? "What are we going to do about the reception now that Charlie's not allowing it at the bar?"

Autumn glanced at Cara and Fran and then back to Rylee as she shook her head. "You were so wrapped up in your own conversation with loverboy that you didn't hear a word I said, huh?"

Rylee's cheeks reddened with a guilty blush as she offered a quick apology. "I'm sorry. Cayden's been talking nonstop about plans for our honeymoon, and I'm just so excited—"

"It's okay," Autumn said, holding up a hand to stop Rylee mid sentence. And even though she didn't really, she still managed to say, "I understand. Everything will be taken care of, and there's nothing for you to worry about other than scheduling your fitting and picking out your flowers."

Rylee's eyes lit up at the mention of dresses and flowers. "My mom and sisters are setting that up as we speak. I hope you don't mind?"

Autumn smiled and checked that portion of *to-dos* from her list. One less thing she had to worry about while she ironed out the finer details of the wedding. "Not at all. I love that they're willing to help."

Rylee's phone rang, taking her attention away from their conversation. Autumn wondered what it would be like on the other side of wedding planning. Being the one getting married instead of being the one planning the wedding.

"Sorry, guys, I gotta take this," she said, waving goodbye as she rushed out of the coffee shop in a hurry.

"I have a few calls to make myself," Autumn said, grabbing her phone off the table and closing her planner. "I'll probably make them from home," she said, "Are we meeting here tomorrow, or are you and Emmalee talking more about the guys and their trip?"

She hadn't meant for the words to come out the way they did. Cara leaned back as though they had slapped her across the face. "Is everything okay?" Her question was full of emotion, but like all things Cara, it was straightforward and to the point. She was never one to beat around the bush.

"Yeah, why wouldn't it be? I didn't—"

"I mean... are *we* okay?"

Autumn felt bad for allowing her insecurities to shine through, causing her best friend to question their friendship and where they stood. She nodded and offered a smile. "Of course we're okay. I'm just stressed out and not sure where to go from here."

"Aww, Autumn," Cara said, pulling her in for another hug. "I'm sorry that everything feels like it's falling apart. Give it time. I'm sure everything will be just fine. You're great at this wedding stuff. There's nothing that could happen to derail you completely off track. You've got this."

Autumn smiled, knowing her best friend was right. There really wasn't much that could knock her off track. Her determination to continue successfully planning weddings was a lot stronger than her greatest weakness—which was currently Charlie—and she wasn't going to allow him to have the final say.

CHAPTER EIGHT

He hadn't forgotten that he'd promised his aunt another visit, but for now he figured it was best to stay away from the coffee shop. He figured it'd give Autumn more time to cool off.

Climbing into the cab of his truck, he turned the key and the engine roared to life. There was nothing quite like the sound of an old diesel farm truck.

Before he had a chance to back out of his driveway, Cayden's car pulled in behind him and blocked him from leaving.

Shifting back into park, he hopped out and met Cayden, who didn't appear too happy. Putting the pieces together, Charlie figured his brother's future wife must have told him all about the war he'd created in the coffee shop the other day. News traveled fast around the small town, and to be honest, he was surprised it had taken as long as it had for Cayden to confront him. *If*, in fact, that was the reason for the unannounced visit.

"What the hell were ya thinkin'?" Cayden asked, confirming Charlie's suspicion. But before Charlie could explain, his brother said, "The bar's a no go for the reception now? Why's that? Because your head's in the wrong place, you're goin' to mess things up for me, too?"

"I'm not messin' anything up," Charlie said matter-of-factly. He wasn't. He had everything under control. Or at least, he *did*. He had expected her to blow up his phone, and if she would have, he could have made things right. He chuckled at the realization he was being a bit immature, but it was all in good fun.

"You don't like *frilly decorations*?" his brother asked, mocking him for being pathetic.

"Come on, I wasn't bein' serious," Charlie admitted, knowing he'd gone too far with saying what he had. The look on Autumn's face had been all the proof he needed. "I was just tryin' to get her attention, is all."

"Is all?" Cayden asked, his shout echoed in the open, surrounding the lake. "You've caused a great deal of stress for someone who's only wantin' attention. You can't be serious."

"It is what it is," Charlie said, knowing his lack of an explanation was only making things worse, and by the look on Cayden's face, he was either going to sock him a good one or…

"You either make things right and put the bar back on the table, or you're not comin' to the wedding."

He couldn't help but laugh. This had gone too far. And though he hated to admit that he acted like an immature idiot, it was now his brother who was taking the title.

"Why are you laughin'? This isn't funny."

"You can't kick me out of your weddin' just because I'm not allowin' a frilly reception at the bar. This has nothin' to do with us."

Running a hand through his hair, and nearly pulling it out, Cayden shook his head and blew out a deep breath. "I can't believe this," he said, talking to himself as he looked out over the lake. Turning back in Charlie's direction, he said, "You're bein' serious right now?"

Charlie shook his head with a half laugh. "No, for Pete's sake, calm down before you have a coronary."

"Well, come on, you've got the whole coffee shop talkin', and Rylee's all worried that everything's goin' to hell in a handbasket. And here you are, laughin' about it."

"I'll call Autumn and make things right." He said the words without thinking them through. Calling her was the last thing he wanted to do. And he was sure that seeing his number pop up on her phone was the last thing she would want right now. It was best to leave well enough alone.

"I don't think that'd be a good idea either," Cayden said, shaking his head with a chuckle. Obviously he had the same thought Charlie did about how Autumn would react to him calling her. Knowing her, she wouldn't answer. Instead, she'd make him the laughing stock of the town he grew up in. "Look, as long as I know we're still on for the bar, I'm not going to worry about it. I'll tell Rylee not to worry, either."

Charlie nodded, knowing by this time next week they'd be on their fishing trip and all of this would be history. "You've got my word."

"Good. Shake on it?" Cayden asked, extending his hand in Charlie's direction, leaving him with one of two choices—shake on it or get kicked out of the wedding.

He grabbed hold of his brother's hand and shook it. "But don't be tellin' Rylee that we had this conversation. I'll tell Autumn myself."

"Deal."

Arriving at the bar, he decided to get a few things done outside before heading in. He needed to trim up the bushes lining the deck overlooking the creek out back, and the grass was a foot taller than he'd like it. A good hour or two spent outside would be enough time to get the property up to par.

He grabbed his keys and his phone, glancing at the screen one last time before shoving it into the front pocket of his Levi's. He had expected her to call the day he'd left the coffee shop, when she was more than ticked off and throwing daggers at him. A part of him knew if she hadn't called then, she wouldn't be calling now, but that still didn't stop him from checking his phone. Just a case of wishful thinking.

"Hey." His sister, Catie, came up from behind him. "I thought I'd catch you here sooner or later."

"Hey, how are things goin'?"

He didn't see Catie as often as he used to, especially since she took ownership of the rundown bed and breakfast across town. She hadn't been working on it like she'd planned because the bank wasn't allowing her to take a loan out to fix the place up. If he hadn't invested his entire savings into his bar, he would have gladly handed her the money without hesitation.

Seeing his family chasing dreams and achieving them was something he'd never get tired of. The Mitchells were a prominent name in Maple Glen. It wasn't a secret that they owned the majority of the land and the businesses in town, but that didn't mean they were greedy. They'd give the shirt off their backs and the food on their plates if it meant helping the people in the community.

After a minute of hesitation, Catie said, "It's goin'. Not so great, but I guess it could be a lot worse, right?"

He nodded, wondering what was really going on. She didn't seem too bothered by whatever it was, but she had always been good at pretending everything was all right. "That's right," he said, offering her a nudge to make her smile. "What brings you this way? I might put ya to work if you've got nothin' better to do."

She took a step back and waved her arms as she shook her head. "Oh no, I've got plenty to do of my own. I was just stoppin' by on my way to the hardware store. I've got a list a mile long and it won't shop for itself."

"The bank finally give you the loan?" he asked, not wanting to pry or involve himself in her business, but he wanted to celebrate with her once the bank finally did decide to give her the money.

A frown crossed her face, and she looked off in the distance away from him, telling him she was trying to keep her emotions in check.

"Hey, it's okay," he said, offering a side hug as she nodded. "The timin' just isn't right. Give it a bit longer, and you'll have the money in no time."

She swiped an escaped tear from her cheek and nodded. "The loan officer told me they'd like to see the turnaround before they make a final decision. But they don't understand that you can't make money when the place looks like it does. It needs a lot of work. People don't want to stay at a place that looks like a dump."

He understood where she was coming from. She made a good point. But at the end of the day, banks didn't care about all that. They only cared if their investment would put money back in their pockets or not.

"Give it time, sis," he said, checking his phone out of habit. "If I find some spare time, I'll be sure to stop by and help out with what I can."

"Thanks," she said, wiping a few more stray tears away.

"That's enough about me and my craziness. Let's talk about yours."

He tipped his head back laughing and asked, "What about mine?"

"I hear you've caused quite the war?"

"Maybe?"

"Aunt Fran said you were called a sexist pig?" Catie asked, blocking the sun from her eyes as she looked over at him. "Never in a million years would I have thought a woman would call you that."

He chuckled and shrugged. "It surprised me, too."

Laughing, Catie shook her head and said, "I also heard that she likes you. Like, a lot."

"You'll have that," he said, a smug grin on his face.

"Cut it out," she demanded, slapping his arm. "You can't be single for the rest of your life, ya know?"

"Who says?"

He dodged another slap as he darted in the opposite direction while she attempted to chase him around his truck.

She stopped in front of his truck, looking over the hood at him. "Look me in the eye and tell me that you don't like her."

Laughing, he made his way to the front of the truck and leaned on the hood. There was no way he could do what his sister asked of him. So instead, he came clean. Telling her what he feared the most and how being friends had seemed like a good idea until it wasn't. He didn't have anything to worry about now that he'd crossed the line and made an enemy out of her. But he couldn't help wondering what it'd be like to call her his wife someday.

"You think I'm crazy?" he asked, looking her square in the eye and waiting for the truth.

"Not really, no. But I'd think you'd be crazy if you don't make things right before it's too late," she said, pushing off the hood of his truck and landing on her feet. "I'm not one to know all about findin' *the one* because my time hasn't come yet, but I do know that if you think she's the one, you'd be an idiot to let your fear of fallin' ruin your chances with her."

He nodded as she said goodbye and headed back in the direction she'd come from. She was right, and he knew it. His fears were just that—fears, not truths. He couldn't allow his weaknesses to become a barrier to his happiness. He needed to find a way to make it work. He'd start by asking her to forgive him.

CHAPTER NINE

"What in the—" Autumn grabbed her phone off the table and looked at the text message glaring back at her. She hadn't drank enough coffee yet to think straight, but after reading the message again, it was obvious what was going on. "Who does he think he is?"

"Who?" Emmalee asked as she took a long drink of her iced coffee. Before Autumn had a chance to tell her, she nodded and set her coffee down. "Oh, nevermind. I know who. What'd he say?"

Autumn looked over her shoulder, checking to see if Cara was still with Vince at a nearby table. *Of course, she was.* Morning coffee talk was continuously interrupted by Vince and Clayton. It was only a matter of time before their coffee time no longer existed.

She tapped her screen and handed it to Emmalee, allowing her to see for herself. Emmalee grabbed the phone and read the message. Her jaw dropped, and she handed the phone back across the table. "Wow. He has a lot of nerve."

"Right? I'm glad I'm not the only one who thinks that," Autumn said, setting her phone down before she made the mistake of responding back to him. She glanced over at the counter, finding Fran finishing up with a customer.

"What are you going to do?"

"Ignore him for now," Autumn said, pulling her wedding planner out of her bag. She needed to think before she reacted. She didn't want to get her hopes up too soon. She'd let him simmer while she debated on giving him another chance.

"Are you sure you'll be able to do that?" Emmalee asked with a light chuckle as she sipped her coffee.

Autumn furrowed her brow. "You don't think I'll be able to?"

Emmalee laughed and pointed over to Fran, who was now preparing another pot of coffee as a new line formed at the counter. "Not if Fran has a say in it."

Autumn shook her head, allowing a soft laugh to escape as she thought about Fran's success rate in Maple Glen. "Of course not, but I've always loved a good challenge."

She was feeling a bit too confident for her own good. She knew better than to believe the words that came out of her mouth when it came to Charlie. Fran's success rate was high, and she honestly didn't see the woman giving up without a fight. Fighting for love seemed a bit over the top, but it was what it was. After all, it was a matchmaker's job, wasn't it?

"Good luck," Emmalee said, sliding to the edge of the booth before standing with a stretch. "She's like a bloodhound when it comes to sensing things around here. And I'm afraid she won't give up that easily."

"That's what I'm afraid of," Autumn mumbled as she watched Emmalee walk toward the counter in search of a refill. She looked back at Cara, who was now saying goodbye to Vince and seeing him out the door. *About time.* The wedding planning was going well, as well as it could in a new town, of course, but she still would like to have her best friend on standby for times like this when she wasn't sure what to do next.

"What'd I miss? Anything good?" Cara asked, upbeat and full of smiles. Autumn was happy for her. She had finally found her true love and happiness in Maple Glen.

Without saying a word, Autumn nodded and handed her the phone. Allowing her to read the text message, Autumn waited to see Cara's reaction.

Her eyes widened as she brought a hand to her mouth and said, "When did he send this?"

"Not too long ago," Autumn said, taking her phone back and reading the message again for the fifth time. "Is he serious?"

Cara slid in across from Autumn, making room for Emmalee and Fran as they approached the booth. "It's hard to say, but maybe he had a come-to-Jesus moment?"

Laughter erupted between them. Sharing a laugh with Cara felt good. Fran slid into the booth, sharing a side with Autumn just as Autumn said, "I'm not sure what to do… or even say."

"What happened now?" Fran asked, pouring sugar into her coffee and stirring it in. "Is this about who I think it's about?"

"He sent me a message," Autumn said. She once again offered her phone as evidence before saying, "He wants me to forgive him. He says he didn't mean to be a jerk and cause a ruckus."

"A ruckus? That's what he called it?" Fran asked, chuckling as she looked down at Autumn's phone displaying the message.

"His words, not mine," Autumn said with a laugh. "As far

as I'm concerned, he meant everything he said, and he's just apologizing because he's in hot water."

Laughing, Fran shook her head and handed the phone back to Autumn, but Cara grabbed it and read the message once again. "I think he means it, though," she said, handing the phone over and glancing at Fran. "Don't you think so, Fran?"

"Well, either he's sittin' in hot water like Autumn says and is feelin' the heat, or he's sincere and feelin' bad for bein' such a... what'd ya call him?" Fran asked, snapping her fingers as Autumn said, "A sexist pig?"

"A sexist pig. That's it," Fran said with a laugh as she tipped back her coffee mug and raised her brows in Autumn's direction. Setting the cup back down, she said, "I honestly hope it's the latter of the two. He's a good man, Autumn."

"Yeah, well, I guess we'll see," Autumn said, finally deciding to send him a text message back.

She couldn't stay mad at him. Whether he was sincere or not with his apology, she would find out sooner or later. They'd shared a connection right off the bat, and that was hard to walk away from.

"I hate to run, but duty calls," Emmalee said, waving goodbye before heading out the door. The deli was to open in less than thirty minutes, and Autumn knew that business had picked up since Scott and Linda's retirement. It was a good sign that things in the small town were going strong. It gave her a lot of hope for her own business.

"Speakin' of Charlie and the whole conniption fit he had about the wedding reception," Fran said, shaking another packet of sugar into her coffee. "How's the rest of the plannin' goin'?"

"Great," Autumn said, glancing at the list of things left to do for Cayden and Rylee's wedding. There were several things marked off, but some of the larger items were still needing to be taken care of. It was helpful to know that Rylee's mother and sisters were helping where they could. And as long as those things were taken care of and done right, Autumn wouldn't have a problem. "We're less than a month or so out, and things are falling into place. She has some help from her family too, so as long as they're fine with it, so am I."

"Say," Fran said, tapping her thumbs along the rim of her mug, "you girls wouldn't happen to know anything about that bake sale this weekend at the festival, would ya?"

To be honest, Autumn had forgotten all about the festival. It seemed like it had been mentioned weeks ago, but had it really only been a few days?

Chuckling, she said, "I honestly have no idea. I've been so focused on this wedding stuff that I forgot all about it. Do you know anything about it, Cara?"

Cara had been silent for the last thirty minutes, and it was obvious she was caught up in another conversation happening elsewhere as her fingers tapped furiously against her phone's screen. "Huh? What?"

Setting her phone down, she looked over at Fran and Autumn. "I'm sorry, I'm having a nice little chat with someone—"

"Well, now wait a minute," Fran said, tapping her fingers against the table. "I thought this was girl talk over coffee in the mornin's. Who on earth has your attention? I'd like to have a word with them about takin' my girl's attention away from me."

Cara glanced at Autumn and back to Fran. She wasn't going to say who it was she was talking to. Autumn knew it just by the look on her face. More than likely it was one of her brothers, and if Autumn had to guess, she'd say it started with a *C* and ended in an *E*.

"I'm sorry, what were you wanting to know?" she asked, setting her phone face down in front of her and offering them her attention. Autumn chuckled as she wondered how long before Cara picked it up again.

"There's a bake sale at the festival on Saturday, and I'm just wonderin' if you've heard anything more about it."

Cara looked at Autumn, who in turn shook her head with a shrug of her shoulders. "I didn't know about a bake sale, but I do know there's a contest of some sort happening after noon."

"Huh," Fran said, leaning back as she crossed her arms. "I bet that's what it was I heard the gossip queens talkin' about."

"Gossip queens?" Autumn asked, knowing exactly who Fran was referring to. "Aren't you a part of that group?"

Fran tipped her head back and let out a loud laugh. "Oh honey, of course not. I just pretend to be so I can get the inside scoop around here."

"Whatever you say, Aunt Fran," Cara said, looking down at her phone, and Autumn could tell how badly she was itching to pick it up and check it. Cara glanced back up at them and said, "I hate to cut this short, but I've gotta go."

"Is everythin' alright with Vince?" Fran asked, looking out the large bay window beside them and checking for any sign of something going on. Autumn was new to town, but one thing she knew for sure was Maple Glen hardly ever experienced chaos and destruction. She knew Vince was the deputy, newly promoted to having a K9 unit, but still, there was no worry that something was wrong.

"Yes, everything is fine with him. I just need to get a few things done. Mark a few errands off my list for the day, is all."

Before leaving, she gave Autumn a hug and told her that she'd catch up with her later. They needed to go over a few details involving the picture taking, but that could wait.

"What in the world was that all about?" Fran asked Autumn, clearing the table of empty mugs.

"Your guess is as good as mine," Autumn said without a clue. She could only imagine it involved Charlie, or maybe she was wrong and it didn't involve him at all.

She gathered her planner and notebooks, shoving them into her bag and zipping it closed. It was going to be a nice day outside with weather in the low sixties, and there wasn't a cloud in sight. Gorgeous fall weather was her weakness, making it hard to stay indoors.

"I'll see you tomorrow, Fran?" she called out on her way to the door with her bag slung over one shoulder.

"I'll be here," Fran said as she grabbed a broom and dustpan near the counter. "Unless, of course, a *Prince Charmin'* comes and sweeps me off my feet."

"You never know," Autumn said, opening the door and looking back at Fran. "Anything's possible here in Maple Glen, right?"

"That's right, dear," Fran said with a wink and one last wave. "You just never know."

Autumn was halfway to her car when her phone rang. She had just enough time to dig it out of her bag and answer it on the fourth ring.

"Hello?" she answered without paying any mind to who it was.

"Autumn?"

"Charlie?"

CHAPTER TEN

Taken by surprise that she actually answered, he was at a loss for words. Everything he'd planned to say went with the breeze as he leaned against the bar's porch railing.

"I didn't expect you to answer," he said, sounding like an idiot. He was telling her the truth. He really hadn't expected her to answer when she realized it was him calling. "Are you busy?"

The last thing he wanted to do was hold her up. If she had places to go and things to do, he didn't want to keep her waiting.

"No, not really," she said, keeping her answer short and sweet. He heard the hesitation in her voice. He knew he'd caused her to rethink everything when it came to him, but he wanted to reverse the damage. *His* damage. The damage he'd created just because he was scared of falling in love with her. "Actually, I was just leaving Fran's Coffee when you called. Now I'm sitting in my car wondering what it is you want."

Her snarky response made him laugh. She was feisty, and he liked that about her. She didn't take crap from anyone.

That was a good thing. It meant she wouldn't take crap from him, either. So he needed to get it together. *Soon.*

"Well, when you put it like that," he said, pushing off the railing and walking toward the other end of the porch. "I want to know if I can have another chance?"

"Another chance?" Her question, though it sounded full of cynical confusion, offered a tinge of excitement and hope. He often read between the lines and waited to be proved wrong. "Like we're playing Yahtzee and you don't want to take a zero?"

He held the phone away from his ear and looked at it. Where the heck did this girl come from? She had jokes and thought she was cute?

Laughing, he pressed the phone back against his ear. "Yeah, I guess so."

"So... this is your way of saying that I can have the frillies at the reception?"

Running a hand through his hair, he said, "About that—"

"How about that zero?" she teased.

"Okay, fine," he said, shaking his head even though she couldn't see him. "I was just going to tell ya that I wasn't serious about all of that anyway."

"Wait, what?"

"I just wanted you to say somethin' to me, and at that moment, anything was better than nothin'," he admitted, knowing she was more than likely having second thoughts about answering the call.

"You can't be serious," she finally said a short time after a deadly silence. "You... Charlie... "

"I'm sorry?" As he said it, he cringed as he waited for her to tell him off.

But as soon as she laughed and said, "I can't believe you.

I think you're going to have to take that zero now," he knew their fight had ended.

"No, but seriously," he said, laughing along with her. "I didn't mean to make you mad. Actually, I have to admit I was kinda scared."

"Scared? Of me?"

"Yeah, I mean, aside from *sexist pig* and other names you called me," he said with a chuckle at the memory, "those daggers you threw with your eyes were deadly."

"Ha ha, yeah, I've heard I have a fatal glare."

"You do," he said, thinking of how mad he'd made her. "Can I tell you somethin', though?"

"Sure?" she said with a nervous laugh.

"You're cute when you're mad, but I promise to never make you *that* mad again."

Her laughter echoed into the phone, and he couldn't help but laugh with her. He knew it was a rueful attempt to make her forgive him, but it was working.

"I wouldn't go that far," she said, chuckling. "That's a complicated promise to keep for someone like you."

"Someone like me?" he asked, jabbing a finger into his chest. Of course, she couldn't see him, but if she could have, he would have wanted her to see his puppy dog eyes and soft pout. "I don't make promises I can't keep."

"I guess we'll have to wait and see about that."

"Okay, I promise to make you smile from this day forward," he said, standing straight and tall as he concentrated on every word he was about to say and making sure to get them right the first time. "When you're upset, call me. When you're stressed, call me. When you're having a bad day, or even a good day, call me. I'll be here for you. I promise."

"Charlie," she asked with a soft sniffle, "is that you?"

"Yes, it's really me," he said, smiling like a buffoon. "Now, do I get my second chance?"

"Yes."

"Yes?"

"Yes, Charlie, you get another chance," she said, and he could hear the smile in her voice. "Just don't mess it up this time, okay?"

"I promise I won't," he said, fist pumping the air as he danced in a circle on the back porch. "But let me ask you one thing first."

"What's that?"

"Will you go out with me tonight?"

"To the bowling alley?"

"What if it was? Would that change your answer?"

Laughter echoed on the other end of the phone line, and it was music to his ears. Things were back to being good between them, and he couldn't wait to see what happened next.

"I'd love to."

"That's good, because I'm not takin' you there," he said, smiling widely and hoping she'd love the place he had in mind.

"Then where *are* you taking me?" Her question was full of skepticism and excitement. He loved it.

"You'll see," he said, refusing to give her any hints. "Can you be ready by seven?"

"Yes, *if* you tell me where we're going."

"Seven it is. I'll see ya then."

He hated leaving her in the dark, but it added anticipation, and he couldn't wait to see her reaction.

∼

Pulling into a vacant spot right outside Autumn's apartment building, Charlie checked the time, making sure he wasn't running late. He was right on time. Shutting the truck off, he glanced in the rearview mirror once more.

He'd never cared about his appearance until he met Autumn. He grinned at his reflection. Grabbing his truck keys, he climbed out. He couldn't wait to see her. It felt like it had been an eternity since the last time he'd seen her, and even if it hadn't been but a few days, it was still too long.

Shaking off the negative thoughts, and cursing himself for almost ruining a good thing, he climbed the stairs to the second floor apartment that Autumn now resided in. He'd only been there a few times, with the majority of those times being when he went to see his sister after she'd first moved back to Maple Glen.

Approaching the door and preparing to knock, he realized he forgot the one thing he shouldn't have on the bench seat of his truck. Sprinting down the hallway, he raced down the stairs and headed for his truck.

Swinging open the driver's side door, he leaned in and grabbed the bouquet of flowers he'd picked up from the flower shop on his way to her place. He couldn't take her out empty handed. Even if he was starting from square one all over again and being *just* a friend. He smiled at the thought as he raced back inside, more than ready to get the night started.

Rapping his knuckles against the solid oak door of her apartment, he waited for the feisty brunette with plum-colored lips and dark brown eyes to greet him. He would be lying if he said he wasn't the slightest bit attracted to her. Pulling off the whole *just friends* thing would be difficult, but it was best to take things slow. Especially now that he was working on his second strike.

Music blared from somewhere inside, causing him to

wonder if maybe she hadn't heard his first attempt at knocking. Holding tight to the flowers in one hand, he knocked once again with his free hand. This time, he knocked harder, wondering if her neighbors would open their doors and check to see who was knocking so loudly on Autumn's door.

The music stopped, and he could hear fumbling of something inside the apartment. Footsteps made there way to the door, and he heard the unhooking of the chain before it swung open. "Hey," she said, her eyes widening at the sight of the flowers. He hadn't known which ones to get her, so he'd grabbed the assortment and hoped for the best. He would learn more about her soon enough, including what her favorite flowers were. "Are those for me?"

He nodded as he held them out to her. "Of course they're for you. Who else would they be for?"

Taking them, she raised them to her nose and inhaled the wild scent of mother nature. "Thank you," she said, looking up at him through the flowers. "They're beautiful, but you really didn't have to—"

"Don't," he said, interrupting her before she could ramble off all the reasons he shouldn't have. She could give him a hundred reasons not to buy her flowers, and he would still find the one reason he should—and did. "I wasn't sure what your favorite flower was, but I smelled these and thought you might like them."

With her nose still planted in the center of the flowers, she smiled and said, "I love them. Before we leave, I need to find a vase or something to put them in."

"Okay," he said, taking a step further inside as she walked toward the kitchen in search of a vase. He watched as she dug through her cabinets. "Should I have brought a vase along?"

Continuing her mad search for a vase, she shook her head. "No, there's gotta be one around here somewhere. Cara used to always get flowers from Vince. She had a dozen vases stashed throughout the apartment at one time."

He chuckled while checking the time on his watch without making it obvious.

"I'm sorry," she said, walking past him as she headed for yet another area of the apartment. "Are we going to be late?"

"No need to apologize," he said, leaning against the counter as he waited for her to come back out of what he assumed to be her bedroom. "Why don't you just put them in a glass for now? Do you have one that's tall enough?"

He turned toward the cabinets and opened a few doors until he found what he was looking for. Pulling a tall plastic cup off the shelf, he filled it with tap water and placed it in the center of the counter. "There," he said, motioning for her to put the flowers in the cup of water. "That'll do for now."

She inserted the flowers into the cup and smiled. "Why didn't I think of that?"

He shrugged, and with a smile, he said, "Maybe because you were too focused on finding an actual vase? Sometimes we search for things when the obvious is right in front of us."

She scrunched her nose and laughed. "Since when did you become a man of wisdom?"

He straightened away from the counter, standing tall and confident as he said, "I've always been a man of wisdom. I'd like to think of myself as the next—"

"Stop right there," she said, holding up a hand in front of him. "We need to get going. We don't have time to hear your made-up stories."

Tossing his head back with a laugh, he feigned offense. "Ouch. Tell me how you really feel."

She reached for her purse, slinging the strap over her shoulder and heading for the door. "I thought we had a date to get to."

His eyes widened as he followed her out the door. "Wait a minute," he said, stopping right behind her as she locked the door behind them. She fumbled her keys into her purse before zipping it shut, keeping her eyes focused on the task at hand. "Did you just call this a date?"

Her eyes widened before looking up at him from her purse. Allowing it to fall to her side, she shrugged and said, "Maybe."

"So, does that mean—"

"Don't press your luck, mister," she said with a wagging finger.

He held his hands up in front of his chest and shook his head while he grinned. "I'm not sayin' a word."

Laughing, they walked out of the apartment building and headed for his truck. Whether tonight counted as an actual date or not, it was yet to be determined, but so far things were off to a better start.

CHAPTER ELEVEN

Climbing into the passenger seat of Charlie's truck with his assistance, she noticed he hadn't taken his eyes off of her since arriving at her apartment.

She had made sure to dress in something casual and cute, but comfy. She didn't trust him to not take her to the bowling alley once again. Not that she'd complain because she'd enjoyed herself the last time.

Wearing her hair in curls and pressed back in barrettes had been Cara's idea, and for once she agreed that she looked sophisticated with her hair in curls. She almost looked like a teacher or a super cute librarian, minus the glasses, of course.

Waiting for him to hop in, she fastened her seat belt and checked her reflection in the visor's mirror, currently blocking the setting sun's glare.

"Ready?" he asked as he turned the key in the ignition, allowing the old truck to fire up and rumble to life. There was something about a diesel truck that she'd always liked. And now, it was an added bonus to know the man driving it.

She smiled at her thoughts and nodded. "I'm ready for you to tell me where we're going."

"I don't think so," he said, placing his arm across the seat as he reversed the truck out of the non-parking spot. She couldn't help but notice that it was the same spot Cara had earned her first parking ticket. "You'll have to wait and see."

"So you've said," she said with a smile, looking at him in his flannel shirt and light blue jeans. She remembered the first time she'd met him at his bar. He had been wearing a flannel much like the one he was currently wearing, and not to mention he'd been wearing the same cologne she was smelling now. It was a mix of fireside wood and something she couldn't quite put a finger on, but he smelled good. Almost too good. "How many flannel shirts do you own?"

Taking his eyes off the road as he drove them to their unknown destination, he smirked. "That was random."

She shrugged. She was known to be random, pulling things out of thin air and coming up with something to talk about in times like now. "I'm pretty random, but seriously, how many flannels do you own?"

"Not enough," he said, grinning like a fool as he looked back at the road before them. "Why? Do you have somethin' against my flannels?"

Laughing, she shook her head. He'd gone from kidding around to straight up seriousness in two seconds flat. She made a mental note to never say anything bad about his darn flannel shirts. "Not at all."

He guided the truck along a back road, still keeping their destination on the down low. She wondered what could possibly be located this far out of town, in the middle of nowhere. "Good, because I've got plenty where this came from," he said, plucking at his shirt and laughing. He was definitely full of himself, something she noticed about him when they'd first met all those months ago. She liked a man who had confidence but still questioned things. Cocky, but not over-the-top with arrogance. Was that even possible?

"I'm sure you do," she said, taking one more playful jab at him. "Let me guess, you've got a closet full of cowboy boots, too?"

His deep chuckle turned into a grunt as he guided the truck down another back road. Trees passed by in the blink of an eye as they headed into the wide open space outside of Maple Glen.

"Cowboy boots?" he asked, gripping the truck's steering wheel as they drove along the coarse, gravel road. "Aren't those for cowboys?"

"I don't know, are they?" She had no idea. She was a city girl, born and raised. She hadn't the slightest clue who wore what in small towns like Maple Glen. She'd seen a lot of people around town wearing them, but she didn't want to assume what she didn't know. "I just thought—"

"I think you think too much," he teased, offering her a sly wink as he pulled into a parking lot crowded with several other vehicles. The building sat off in its own area, and if she had to guess, they were five or ten miles outside of Maple Glen. "What is this place?" she asked, trying to figure it out just by staring at it. There was a sign on the south side of the building, but she couldn't read it because a tree was blocking her view.

"See, there ya go thinkin' again," he said, climbing out of the driver's seat and making his way to her side of the truck. He opened her door and said, "How about you hop on out and I'll show you what this place is."

He offered his hand, and she gladly accepted as she hopped to the ground. Landing on both feet, she steadied herself against him before taking her first step. "Quite the jump for someone like you," he said, grinning widely as he dodged her glare.

"Someone like me?" she asked, jamming a finger in her chest. "Are you saying I'm short, Charlie Mitchell?"

"Not at all," he said, swinging the door shut behind her. "But you know what they say. If the shoe fits—"

"Shove it up your—"

"Whoa, calm down *feisty one*," he said, holding up his hands in defense. "I was only jokin'."

"You better be," she threatened playfully with a chuckle as she shoved him away from her. "Let's go. You're killing me."

Opening the door, he allowed her to walk in first, and once she stepped inside, she couldn't believe her eyes. The building housed a full-size family event center with so many opportunities for a good time.

"Are you kidding me right now?" She was surprised. "I would have never expected something like this to exist in a small town like Maple Glen."

"To be fair, it's been here a long time," Charlie said, offering her to go first through another set of double doors. "You've been here before, ya know."

She shook her head. She would have remembered coming to a place like this. She couldn't believe her eyes. She felt like a kid in a candy store. "No, I don't think I have."

"You haven't?" he asked, more surprised at her admission than she was at the realization the place existed. "I guess it's a good thing we're here, then."

She stood still, her feet grounded as her eyes swept across her surroundings. Arcade games lit up around them, catching the attention of several kids from across the way. Signs announced specials on mini golf and rock climbing exhibits.

The place was definitely one she'd come back to time and time again.

"Come on," he said, grabbing hold of her arm and tugging her along. "I'll show you around."

She followed behind him, still amazed at all of the things the place offered. Never in her twenty-nine years had she seen anything like it. Sure, Minneapolis had plenty of sport and family event centers, but she'd never ventured to check them out. She never had a reason to. And since she was overly busy with planning weddings and landing clients, she never had time.

In fact, she couldn't believe the workaholic she'd become over the years was taking a break to hang out and waste time while having fun.

Moving to Maple Glen was definitely a good decision on her part. It was allowing her the benefit of escaping her workload while finding her true self. Sure, she had known what she truly wanted in life before moving to town from the city, but she hadn't physically slowed down until moving here.

"What are you thinkin' about?" Charlie asked, pulling her from her thoughts.

"Just about how great this is," she admitted, looking into his hazel eyes for a minute too long before scanning their surroundings.

"You don't get out much, do you?"

When his question would have normally offended her, she took it as a wake up call. She'd cowered into a reclusive state while working long days and nights with back-to-back clients, making sure every last detail regarding their weddings were figured out and nothing would happen unexpectedly.

"I'd like to think that's about to change," she said, accepting it for what it was. It was time she quit working so hard and trying to control every aspect of her life. It was time to go with the flow and let things happen as they would without her micromanaging every detail.

"You think so?" Charlie asked, as if he had doubts that she could honestly let go of her work long enough to enjoy a bit of downtime.

"Yeah, actually, I do," she said, a new bout of confidence washing out her doubts. "And what about you? You're a lot like me when it comes to business, mister. Don't pretend like you're not a workaholic yourself."

A smug grin crossed his face, and he shrugged. "I guess you're right. It's somethin' we should work on together," he offered, a slight smile tugging at his lips as she looked up at him. "You know, since we're friends and all."

"Are we now?"

"I could've sworn that's what this was... a truce of some sort," he said, nudging her as she rolled her eyes. She hated to admit she'd had thoughts of something more transpiring between them, but for now, she... they... needed to take things slow.

"Whatever you say," she said, walking in the direction of the bumper cars. "I think it's because you don't want to get your butt kicked by a girl," she called out, only to turn around screaming when he chased her.

"I'm not afraid to get my butt kicked by a girl," he said, his words coming out through clenched teeth. "Especially not by you."

Her jaw dropped, but she quickly recovered when he said, "I'd probably like it."

She sighed and rolled her eyes, shaking her head as she got in line for the bumper cars. "We'll see about that," she mumbled, knowing he was too far away to hear her.

Climbing into her very own bumper car, she slid the

helmet on and buckled her seat belt. "Get ready to be beat by a girl!"

She smiled when he nodded, wearing that smug, overly confident grin of his own that she was helpless to resist.

Two hours later and the place was closing for the night. She'd had fun and was more than thankful she'd agreed to come along with him. They'd made a great team playing laser tag against another couple as they scored points and won several games. She liked the idea of hanging out there once a week with him, and maybe inviting the others to tag along with them. It'd be fun and a chance to unwind after a week of planning and getting things lined up for the wedding.

She made a mental note to talk to the girls at their next coffee date and set something up. She knew Cara and Vince would be all for it, but with everyone's crazy schedules, they would have to do some adjusting to make it work.

"What are you thinkin' about?" He walked beside her, holding the door open as they left the building that hosted the most fun she'd had in what felt like forever. She couldn't remember a time when she'd let herself have so much fun without worrying about getting things done for work. Weddings were an important part of her life, and her clients depended on her twenty-four seven, it seemed. But, maybe that was because she allowed them to. She made yet another mental note to set a schedule for herself, allowing certain times of the day to be set aside for herself. She deserved to take breaks throughout the day, and not just a few minutes here and there while drinking coffee or having lunch. "Autumn?"

Hearing her name, she stopped walking and turned to face him. "I'm sorry," she said, frowning because it wasn't the first time she'd spaced out and gotten lost in her own thoughts. Heck, she was becoming a pro at it, but she could tell by the furrow of his brow that Charlie wasn't liking it. "I—"

"Autumn." He ran a steady hand through his hair as he looked off in the distance. He was frustrated with her. She didn't like seeing him annoyed with her, but he needed to realize she was aware of it and things didn't change overnight. It was one of many traits she'd tried to change over the years, but instead of shying away from overthinking and spacing off, it was apparent the opposite was happening. "How can you be havin' fun and engaging in conversation with me one minute, and then the next thing I know, I've lost you?"

Sometimes the truth hurt, and right now she didn't know how to answer him. She didn't like diving deep into her issues, and she knew there were plenty. She definitely didn't feel comfortable with interrogation. Not that he was cornering her, forcing her to answer, but still...

"I don't know," she said, realizing the night was coming to an end and she didn't want it to do so on a sour note. She tried to hold back her sarcasm the best she could, but like most times when she felt under attack, she allowed it to defend her. "But it's nothing new. I've been this way my whole life."

"Hey," he said, touching her arm and sending a wave of electricity bolting through her. He must have felt it, too, because no sooner than his fingertips caressed her skin, he dropped his hand back at his side. "I didn't meant to make you feel bad about it. I just can't figure it out, is all. I enjoy talkin' to you, and when you're distracted and in your own world with whatever thoughts you're havin'..."

He cut himself off, refusing to finish his own sentence. She couldn't help but wonder what he was going to say. "I get it," she said, smiling. She may not know what he was about to say, but she understood what he had said. She was a mess and needed to let go of everything holding her back and taking her away from enjoying life.

"Good, because I'm not a man of many words, and I'd hate to say somethin' and have it come out all wrong, ya know?" Charlie smiled and shook his head. "I'd hate to have those daggers flyin' my way over somethin' I've said."

She laughed. "Trust me, there's nothing you could say right now that I wouldn't agree with," she said, looking up at him and watching his eyes focus on hers. His mouth opened as he was about to say something, but he must have thought twice and pressed his lips closed. She shook her head. "I don't even wanna know."

"You're right," he said, nodding with a sly smile. "What do you say we get out of here?"

"And go where?" She wasn't ready for the night to be over. It felt like things were just getting started.

"Oh, um," he said, glancing at his watch then back at her. "I—"

"If you have something else going on, you can take me home, it's okay," she said, not wanting to pressure him into hanging out longer. She could always go home and snuggle up on the couch with some ice cream and watch more *I Love Lucy* reruns. "I just thought we were having a good time and—"

"Don't want the night to end?" His eyebrows raised in fascination with a hint of curiosity.

She nodded with a smile. "Do you feel it, too? Or is it just me? If it's just me, you can take me home and I'll watch—"

"Where would you like to go?"

She glanced around and watched people drive out of the parking lot, leaving them alone and wondering what to do next. She had no idea what to suggest they do or where they should go. She wasn't from around here, and though it'd been a while since she moved to town with Cara, she hadn't ventured out much aside from Fran's Coffee and the deli across the street.

"Tell ya what," he said, reaching for her arm before tugging her along beside him. "I know just the place, and it's not too far from here."

"Karaoke?" She allowed him to surprise her with their next stop, but she hadn't thought he'd bring her to his bar. Not that she was complaining, because she would never say no to a few drinks. And if he expected her to get up on stage and sing along to the words on the screen, she would definitely need more than a few. "What if I told you I don't like to sing?"

"I would tell you that you're full of crap," he said, offering her a fruity drink from behind the counter. She recognized the guy behind the counter as Cara's little brother, Carter, who had just turned twenty-one last year. Actually, the last time she'd been inside Charlie's bar was the night Carter celebrated his twenty-first birthday. "What girl doesn't like to sing?"

She took the drink from his hand and stirred it as she contemplated his question and how to answer it.

"Come on," he said, grabbing a beer from the cooler and motioning for her to follow him. She wasn't so sure about singing in front of everyone. She wasn't the greatest singer. She definitely wasn't the next Reba McEntire or Dolly Parton, even though she did love to pretend she was every now and then. "I'll sing with you."

She tossed her head back with a laugh and wondered if he

honestly thought that would make her change her mind. Then again, it might. "Really?"

"Really," he said, reaching out for her hand that she gladly accepted. "I enjoy singin' a few every now and then."

His wink was enough to persuade her, or maybe it was the drink in her hand. She could sing, right? It wasn't like she would shatter eardrums or anything. Well, not on purpose anyway. She shot back the last of her drink, a final attempt at gathering the courage she would need to perform in front of a bar full of people.

"Okay, what song are we going to sing?"

He shrugged, causing her heart to race. So much for going with the flow and letting go of control. She needed to know. "You don't know? Don't we get to choose which one we sing?"

Everywhere she'd been in the city allowed people to choose their songs. She didn't know if she could sing along with a song she didn't know. What if she messed up?

He stopped, coming face to face with her in front of the DJ and karaoke machine. "What song do you want to sing? I'm sure Jackson will line it up for us," he said, pointing to the man running the show behind the scenes. She let out a deep breath, slowing her heart rate as she smiled at Jackson. "What songs do you have?"

Jackson motioned for her to step around the speakers and scroll through the selection. He had almost every song Autumn could think of, but she was still having a hard time choosing. She thought of songs performed as a duet, but she wasn't finding the right ones.

"Which ones do you have in mind?" Charlie asked, leaning over her shoulder. The smell of his cologne lingered, and it distracted her from her task. "Autumn?"

Snapping back to reality, she stared at the selection on the screen as the music blared from a nearby speaker. Two women were on stage, belting out lyrics full of slurred and stammered lines. "Do you like country music or—"

"Whatever you like."

That wouldn't make the choices any easier, so she silently scrolled through the list until her eyes landed on a few. "These," she said, pointing to the titles and smiling back at Charlie. "Yeah?"

"Yeah."

"Okay, I'll get them lined up," Jackson said, tapping a few buttons on the machine and offering them a thumbs up. "You're up after the next one."

Good. I have plenty of time to run to the restroom. "I'll be right back," she whispered to Charlie, grabbing his arm to steady herself as she walked around the maze of cords and speakers.

"You're not leavin', are ya?" He pressed against her, whispering into her ear. She felt the heat from his body, and a chill ran down her spine. He awakened senses in her that she hadn't felt in a long time. She stepped away from him, instantly feeling the loss of heat. "I gotta run to the restroom real quick."

She was doing the pee-pee dance as she made her way through the crowd of people. Finally making it to the restroom, she pushed through the door and silently prayed she would be able to keep it together tonight. Between the alcohol coursing through her veins and the thrum of attraction she felt toward him, she wasn't sure how long she'd be able to ignore it and stay *just friends* while taking things slow.

Taking care of business and hurrying back to Charlie, she smiled as she approached him next to the stage. He was holding onto their microphones, and once she was at his side, he offered her one. "Are you ready?"

She had never been one to sing in front of anyone—other than Cara and their other friends back home in the city—but how could she tell him *no* now? The look on his face alone did her in, making it more than difficult to tell him not to bother trying to get her on stage. Besides, what was it the younger generation was saying now? *YOLO.*

"Ready as I'll ever be," she said, taking her drink from a side table and tossing it back. A little more liquid courage couldn't hurt. She took hold of his extended hand and allowed him to drag her on stage without a fight. She was looking forward to singing with him.

Nodding once to Jackson, they signaled they were ready. *More than ready.* She smiled at Charlie, wondering if he would later regret hearing her sing... Not that she had a terrible voice, but she knew the songs they'd picked out were... well, they were songs that made a person feel something while singing them.

The beat to "How Do You Like Me Now" by Toby Keith started, and her eyes lit up. Forgetting they were front and center of the bar, the stage fright disappeared and she allowed herself to let it all out and have fun. Charlie sang right along with her, and if she wasn't biased, she would have to admit they sounded pretty dang good together.

According to the thunderous applause surrounding them once the song ended, the bar's patrons agreed with her.

Smiling at Charlie, she saw a spark in his eye that hadn't been there at the beginning of the night. The chemistry they shared from the first time she met him was magnified by the thousands as she stared into those eyes of his.

Taking a quick break to grab another round of drinks, she walked past Charlie and headed straight for the counter. "Take ten?" she asked Jackson, who nodded and smiled back at her on her way by the speakers.

"Hey," Charlie said, attempting to keep up with her through the crowd. She was more than nervous to sing the next song with him. Afraid it would allow emotions to escape that she'd kept deep inside for so long... "Autumn," he said, reaching for her once they arrived at the counter. "Everythin' alright? I think we did awesome back there."

"Yeah... everything's great," she replied, offering a smile before telling Charlie's part-timer what they were drinking.

"Okay, but I feel like somethin's buggin' ya."

She shrugged, not wanting to ruin the vibe of the night. "It's no big deal. It's just the next song, is all."

She loved the next song more than the first, even though the meaning behind it would hit her hard as she sang the lines. Sheryl Crow and Kid Rock couldn't have been a better duo for the song "Picture," and she wasn't sure if she and Charlie could pull it off.

"What about it?" he asked, grabbing his drink from the bartender and turning back to the stage. Instead of following him, she stayed at the counter and wondered what the heck she was even doing. This wasn't the Autumn she'd been her whole life. She had been focused and driven by a career she had been determined to succeed in—which she had, but that was beside the point. And now, here she was recklessly abandoning her *good girl* ways to impress a guy. For what?

"We don't have to sing it," Charlie said. "It's just a song. I'll tell Jackson to play another. It's no big deal."

She looked up at him, and she couldn't help but wonder why she was causing such a wave in their night out together. She loved the song, and no matter how it made her feel about her ex, she wanted to enjoy the night with Charlie.

"No, it's okay," she said, pushing away from the counter to join him on his venture back to the stage.

"Are you sure?" he asked, turning her to face him once

they were next to Jackson's set-up. "I know the song by heart, and I can imagine why you're wanting to avoid it."

She shook her head and said, "Nope, let's do it." She grabbed hold of his hand and pulled him on stage behind her, offering Jackson a nod as they made their way past him.

"It's just a song, right?"

Before he had a chance to answer, the song's beat blared from the speakers and the crowd went crazy with applause and cheers. She felt like a famous person, without security and riches, of course, but still the crowd was loving her and Charlie.

The way he sang his verse caused her to pull herself closer to him. So close in fact, she was nose to nose with him and staring him in the eyes as they wrapped up the song in unison. Sweat trickled down his face, soaking the collar of his flannel shirt, and her eyes couldn't help but follow the trail of sweat.

"Eyes up here, sunshine," he said, a smirk on his face as he stepped back to give them space. The separation left her body begging for him to come closer and buzzing for more contact. "My song's up next if ya want to join the crowd and get yourself another drink?"

"Can I get you anything before you make all these women swoon and wish you were theirs, Mr. Mitchell?" Emphasis on the swooning, because from the spot she was standing, the view was impressive and a tad overwhelming for her feminine parts. Shaking the thoughts from her head, she smiled up at him as he quirked a brow. "Do I sense a bit of... what do they call it these days?"

"I'm not jealous," she said, matter-of-factly. She wasn't. Not in the least. She knew what she could bring to the table, and glancing around the bar a few times, she'd already surveyed potential threats. But she wasn't worried about them. Not anymore. The way he had looked at her while singing...

"I'll take another beer if the offer's still on the table," he said with a wink as he turned on the heels of his boots and headed back to the center of attention. She smiled and shook her head as she made her way in the opposite direction.

Instead of walking back to the stage with his drink, she climbed onto a barstool and watched him. He was in his element. A cool cat with a voice like a natural. He could easily pass for one of those big-time country singers if someone passing through town didn't know any better.

"Huntin', Fishin', and Lovin' Every Day" by Luke Bryan was a good choice for Charlie to sing. He didn't miss a single word, showing the crowd he knew his music and obviously loved the song. It made sense it was one of his favorites. The Mitchell family seemed to talk quite a bit about fishing, and there was no doubt in her mind that Charlie's brothers would have fit right in up there on stage with him tonight.

The song ended, and she watched as Charlie took a bow before heading in her direction. "There's one more song I'd like to sing, if that's okay?" His eyes pierced hers, freezing her to the counter as she leaned against it. Even if she wanted to tell him that she would rather they sing another song together, she nodded with a smile. He smiled with a wink and grabbed his beer.

On his way to the stage, he whispered something to Jackson, causing him to glance over at her with a wide smile while agreeing to whatever Charlie had said as he hit a button and offered a thumbs up.

She wondered what Charlie was up to... until the song she recognized as Lee Brice's latest hit played over the speakers, and Charlie's eyes were aimed directly at her. She shifted in her seat, wanting to dodge his stare, but there was nowhere for her to go. She furrowed her brow at him, curious about what the heck he was up to and wanting to hide as the crowd followed his eyes and landed on her.

Completely embarrassed, but loving the way he sang "Rumor," she asked the bartender for another round. Hormones and alcohol were never a good mix, and the way Charlie was headed, Autumn wasn't sure what would happen next. And, as Charlie sang the words, she realized what it was he was trying to tell her.

Grabbing the shot glass, she tipped it back and slammed it on the counter next to her. She was done for… heart and all.

CHAPTER TWELVE

"I had a lot of fun tonight. Thanks for comin' out with me," Charlie said, offering Autumn a hand while she climbed out of his truck. They sang plenty of songs while on stage in front of familiar faces he'd recognized throughout the night. They'd garnered plenty of attention, too, guaranteeing they'd be the talk of the town.

Autumn grabbed hold of his hand, stumbling forward as her feet hit the ground. "Whoa, easy there," he said with a light chuckle. She'd had a few too many drinks of liquid courage, but she'd told him how much fun she was having throughout the night while he kept a close eye on her. He hated to drop her off and leave her unattended, but he wasn't going to offer to stay. That would seem… what? He shook his head and dug out his phone. "Should I call Cara and see if she can come stay with you tonight?"

"I'm fine, Char," Autumn said, leaning into his side. "Really, I am. I didn't drink *that* much."

He begged to differ, but he wasn't going to argue with her. He'd done enough of that at the beginning of the week. He wanted to enjoy the rest of their time together—down to the last second. *As a friend*, of course. "I don't think she'd mind," he said, trying to get her to agree that having Cara come over would be a good idea. "I mean, of all the people I'd choose to stay with you, besides myself, Cara would be at the top of the list."

Autumn stopped mid-stride and pulled away from him. Her dark brown eyes looked up at him, and even in the dark of the night, he could see the turmoil in them. "You'd stay with me?"

Her question was full of innocence mixed with inebriation. As much as he'd like to stay with her, he knew there would be no way he'd allow himself to. He needed to keep his thoughts straight, and allowing his attraction for her to make decisions wouldn't be good.

But he wanted to make sure she was going to be all right.

"Look, I'll give my sister a call and she can come stay with you, okay?"

Her eyes shifted, looking away from his. He knew what she must be thinking, and if he was right, she'd be wrong. He would stay with her in a heartbeat to make sure she was okay through the night, but he'd been raised better than to take advantage of a woman when they were intoxicated. Not that he would take advantage of her. Never in a million years would he ever do something cowardly like that. He just wanted to make sure whatever happened between them was as intended, for both parties, and not caused by having a few too many at the bar.

"You don't want to?" Again, her question was innocent and her eyes pleaded for him to stay. And those lips of hers… a pout pulled at her bottom lip, making it hard to resist the urge to kiss her.

"That's not it at all," he said, trying his best to make her understand his reasons. "I just don't think it's a good idea, is all."

She looked away once again, this time her eyes locked on the apartment building's front entrance lit up by a solo light fixture. "Because we're just friends."

The way she said it made him question the label they'd given each other.

"I just think it'd be wise if—"

"It's okay," she said, pushing away from him as she turned to walk away. "You can leave."

"Autumn, don't," he said, following her to the front landing of the apartment building. "I didn't mean—"

"I'm fine," she said, smiling back at him as she turned the handle and let herself inside. "I'll see you tomorrow?"

He stood paralyzed by the fear of losing her as he watched her walk up the stairs in the direction of her apartment. He wanted nothing more than to walk in, follow her up those stairs, and stay with her for the night, but he knew better.

Dialing his sister's number, he waited for her to answer and asked her to stay the night with Autumn. Once she agreed, he waited outside until his sister pulled in. He hated to think of what Autumn was thinking, knowing she overthought everything, but there was one thing he was sure of: she would be okay tonight, and they could talk about it tomorrow.

Walking into Fran's Coffee, something he rarely did before Autumn, Charlie listened to the chatter in a nearby booth as he approached the counter.

"You're finally comin' to enjoy the coffee and stay

awhile?" Fran asked, wiping off the counter as she focused her eyes on him. She'd been wanting him to visit more often, hang around the coffee shop and talk like they used to. He felt bad for not spending time with her, but he didn't spend much time with anyone lately.

Hearing Autumn's laugh, he glanced in her direction. Smiling when his eyes locked with hers, she waved and continued on with her conversation. Things had gone well on their last-minute night out together. He'd planned to talk to her today to make sure she wasn't upset with him for leaving her after dropping her off.

"So," Fran said, pulling his attention back to focus on her, "how'd last night go?"

He grabbed a nearby stool and slid it up to the counter. "Good."

He could only stay for a few minutes because he needed to finish packing for the fishing trip he and his brothers had planned for the weekend.

"Only good?" Fran asked, glancing over at Autumn and back to Charlie. "Because that's not what I've heard so far this mornin'."

He looked over his shoulder, realizing that everyone at Autumn's table was now staring at him while he sat and had coffee with Fran. "What'd she say?"

Fran shrugged and turned away from the counter as she busied herself with more cleaning. "Oh you know, just the normal stuff girls talk about after their dates," Fran said, wiping her rag along the groove of the back counter.

"It wasn't an actual *date*," Charlie said, knowing it was silly to deny it. "We're just—"

"Friends," Fran answered for him. "I know. I've heard that more than once already."

He quirked a brow at Fran. She seemed annoyed about the

label he'd placed on him and Autumn. It was only for the best. There was no sense in rushing things just because they were two people attracted to each other with boundless chemistry. "Is there somethin' wrong with that?"

Fran brought her cup to her lips and took a sip while shrugging to answer his question. He knew what she was thinking. She was thinking he was full of crap and beating around the bush. Lying to himself to protect himself from falling too hard and ending up losing out on a good thing. It had happened once before, and there wasn't anything to say it wouldn't happen again. He was better to play it safe than to be sorry later.

Besides, Autumn was Cara's best friend. He'd heard stories about what happened between siblings and their friends when things went south in the relationship. He and Cara weren't the closest siblings, but still, family meant something more to him than most guys would care to admit.

"Do you think there's somethin' wrong with it?" Fran asked, bouncing his question back at him even though she already knew the answer.

"No," he answered, setting his cup down and glancing back at Autumn. "I don't."

Fran walked around the counter and pulled up a stool next to him. Leaning on the counter, she wrapped her hands around her coffee mug and said, "Let me ask you somethin'."

He sat up, straightening himself to prepare for whatever she threw his way. "Go for it," he said with a smile. "I'm ready."

"What are you so scared of?"

He gulped and let out a ragged breath. He lied. He wasn't ready. He scanned her eyes, looking for a hint, some kind of clue to let him know that she truly wanted to know the answer to that question.

"I'm not scared," he said, fidgeting with the handle of his cup and avoiding Fran's eyes because in an instant, she'd know he was lying. He couldn't lie to her, or to anyone for that matter. He wasn't even good at lying to himself. Telling himself he didn't want anything more than just friendship with Autumn had been the worst lie of all, and his aunt knew it. Fran folded her arms across her chest and gave him the look that told him he was full of crap. "I'm not."

"Then why didn't you stay with her last night?" Fran asked, holding her gaze steady with his, waiting for him to answer.

"Is that even a question that I need to answer?" He glanced one last time at Autumn, wondering if she felt the same way Fran felt, and if that was the reason for Fran asking him about it. "I didn't stay the night with her because she wasn't sober, and I wasn't going to take a chance on screwin' things up with her."

"So you do want somethin' more than just friends, huh?" Fran said, the sly smirk on her face telling him that he should have known better than to trust her line of questioning. Being interrogated by Fran was something he should have been prepared for, but once again, he stepped right into her trap and allowed her to put the pieces together. "You're a good man, Charlie," she said, finishing off her cup of coffee before sliding off her seat. "You've always been one to do the right thing, and last night was no different. Good for you to look out for one another like that. Integrity looks good on you. But, I still think love would look good, too."

She patted his arm as she walked by, heading in the direction of the booth taken by Autumn and the rest of the coffee gang. He wanted to follow Fran over to the booth and invite himself to sit down with Autumn. He wanted to pick up where they left off last night, this time without alcohol involved, of course, and make sure they were okay. Even if the smile on her face told him things were okay, he wanted to hear her say it.

Glancing at his phone, he realized he was running behind schedule. He needed to get home and get things ready for the trip with the guys. If he didn't get his butt in gear, there was a chance they would leave him behind. And after hiring a part-time bartender for the nights and weekends he'd be away, he could afford to go on a vacation. Besides, he had a lot of catching up to do with his brothers and future brothers-in-law.

Offering a quick wave to Autumn, he headed for the door and made a mental note to call her later.

CHAPTER THIRTEEN

She watched Charlie leave the coffee shop, offering a quick wave on his way out the door. She couldn't help but wonder if he would have sat down and talked to her if she hadn't been surrounded by the girls.

"What's new with you?" Fran asked, sliding in next to Autumn. "A little birdie told me that the two of you had a lot of fun last night."

Autumn glanced over at Cara, who held her hands up and shook her head. "It wasn't me."

"This time," Autumn said with a half laugh before looking back at Fran. "What'd he say?"

Fran smiled before taking a drink of her coffee. "Who's to say it was Charlie who told me?"

"Who else is there?" Autumn asked, looking at Emmalee and Rylee, who, like Cara, shook their heads and shrugged their shoulders.

"Let's just say that I've got friends and they tell me things," Fran said with a chuckle.

"Okay, but still," Autumn said, trying to figure out who would have mentioned it to Fran about her and Charlie's night out together. "Not everyone knows about us or what's going on between us."

Fran shook her head, grabbed her coffee and said, "I think you've forgotten where you're at, dear. This is a small town you're livin' in now. Everyone knows everythin', whether you'd like them to or not."

How could Autumn forget. She hadn't really, she'd just been so caught up in making ends meet and planning Rylee and Cayden's wedding, she hadn't paid much attention to anything else. Of course it was a small town. And of course people were going to talk. How many people had seen her and Charlie last night, hanging on each other and having a good time among the crowd? Too many to count. It didn't help that they were in Charlie's bar *and* surrounded by people who knew him. That alone was enough to tell her exactly what she needed to know.

"Anyway, it's not that big of a deal," Autumn said, waving it off as she checked her phone for missed calls or messages. Nothing yet. She thought about sending him a message, asking to meet up for lunch after a while, but decided to wait and check back in an hour after she got some things squared away with Rylee about the wedding. The countdown was on, and they needed to stay focused. *She* needed to stay focused.

"It's not?" Fran asked, chuckling as Autumn rolled her eyes and grabbed her planner and a pen. "I'm just givin' you a hard time, dear. I think you two are cute together."

"So do I," Cara said, offering Autumn a wink from across the table. Autumn furrowed her brow and feigned annoyance. Honestly, she liked the fact that everyone was okay with her and Charlie. Even if he ended up leaving her alone last night after dropping her off. Well, technically not alone, because he did call Cara and had her stay with Autumn to make sure she was okay through the night. Which, if she were to be honest, was something she wasn't used to. Either the guy stayed and tried to take advantage of her inebriated state of mind, or he took off without a care for her well being. Either way, Charlie wasn't anything like the guys in her past. Charlie was a decent human being and a good friend. *Friend.* It seemed so weird to call him that, but it was what it was. For now.

"Okay, anyway, enough about me and Charlie," Autumn said, thumbing through the pages of her planner. Looking at her scribbled notes along the side of the page, she realized she'd forgotten to call the bakery and schedule the cake to be made. "We've got planning to do, *if* you don't mind?"

Her question and eyes were directed at everyone gathered around the table. Some, like Emmalee and Fran, didn't have to stick around and figure things out, but then again, the more the merrier. If they were willing to toss out ideas and help out wherever they could, Autumn wouldn't mind it one bit. Not that she couldn't handle it all on her own, because she'd done plenty of weddings in the city, much larger than Cayden and Rylee's, and had received no complaints while her clients offered her compliments of a job well done.

"With everything going on, I forgot to order the cake," Autumn admitted, hearing a slight gasp from Rylee, who snapped her jaw shut once Autumn looked her way. "It's no big deal, really. There's still plenty of time to get it ordered and set up for the wedding."

"They weren't kiddin' when they said you were distracted and caught up in him," Cara teased, wiggling her eyebrows in Autumn's direction. Autumn scrunched her forehead at Cara, a look that would become permanent if she didn't stop.

Tossing her hands up, Autumn dropped her pen on the pad of paper in front of her. "I just want to know who *they* are, and if *they* know so much about me, maybe *they* should tell me," Autumn said in a huff, "because it's obvious *they* know more about what's going on than I do. And I'd love to at least have an idea, if not a little hint as to what in the world I'm getting myself into."

Cara laughed, causing Emmalee to warn her with a wave of her hand to cut her off. Autumn looked at Emmalee, who sat there in silence with an innocent smile across her face. Of course, everyone played innocent when they were anything but. She had a feeling Emmalee and Clayton were talking, along with Vince and Cara. It didn't help matters that Charlie had called Cara to come to the rescue of the *drunk girl* who couldn't handle herself. *Lies.* She would have been just fine without Cara being there. Instead of going right to sleep, she had wanted to binge watch her favorite show while eating day-old doughnuts from the bakery with Charlie next to her on the couch. But instead, Cara had tucked her in, provided her with a puke bucket beside her bed, and told her to get some sleep. She'd done anything but sleep as she tossed and turned, wondering why he hadn't wanted to come inside with her.

"Earth to Autumn," Cara said, waving a hand in front of her face. "Are you done, or would you like to tell us how you really feel?"

Autumn sighed, picked up her pen, and flipped her notebook over. "I'm done."

She scribbled notes and reminders for herself. Little to-dos for the week ahead of her. The festival was this weekend, and since the week had dragged on forever and an eternity, she was more than ready to get out and about while finding something that didn't involve planning for a wedding, or hearing the latest gossip—which now involved her. She wondered how long the gossip would last until *they* moved on to the next unsuspecting person in town.

"Is there anything you'd like me to do?" Cara asked, grabbing her own notebook and pen. "I can call the bakery and line up the cake to be prepped and ready for the big day. Or I can call and order samples of invitations? Anything you want me to do, just let me know," Cara said, stealing a sip of coffee from Autumn's cup. "I'm ready."

"Just make sure your camera is ready," Autumn said, laughing as she feigned annoyance.

"You know that it's always ready," Cara said, stealing yet another drink of Autumn's coffee.

"Fran, will you please get her some coffee of her own so she stops stealing mine?" Autumn asked, laughing as Fran nodded and slid out of the booth. "Rylee, have you decided on your wedding colors? Have you found a dress?"

Rylee's eyes widened and she shook her head. She looked like she was about to open the flood gates if Autumn didn't say something soon. "It's okay, I just need to know so I can continue on with decorations and other planning," Autumn said, assuring the poor thing that everything was going well and they still had plenty of time. "Do you have a favorite color?"

Rylee, who most of the time wore dark colors and different shades of pink, shrugged. Autumn wondered if she should mention black and pink for the wedding colors, but decided to wait it out. Time would tell, hopefully sooner rather than later. "I don't really have a favorite, but I do like pink."

"Perfect," Autumn said, scribbling inside her planning notes.

"But..." Rylee said, fidgeting with her fake fingernails as she waited for Autumn to look up from her notebook. "Cayden doesn't like pink."

Autumn looked at Cara for clarification, and she

shrugged, obviously not knowing much about Cayden's likes and dislikes. "Well, what if you had pink and black for your colors? We can make the arrangements on the table look adorable with lilies and black ribbons, along with some other cute things I have in mind."

Rylee shook her head. "I don't think I want black to be in my wedding colors," she said matter-of-factly, looking between Cara and Autumn. "Isn't that the color of bad luck or something?"

Autumn held back the disappointment she felt. She glanced at Cara, hoping she'd be able to read Autumn's silent expression. So much for everything going so well. This was the moment she'd been waiting for. The moment the shoe dropped and either everything was a *no* or the bride to be became *Bridezilla* with a capital *B*.

Cara chuckled, and Autumn knew what her best friend was thinking. She was thinking it, too. Like where in the world did Cayden find this woman? Not that Rylee was a bad person for being naïve... was that even the right word to use to describe her? She wasn't naïve all the time, that was the good thing. But right now, Autumn wanted to grab the woman's shoulders and tell her to figure things out.

They had just over a month, and not even a few moments ago Autumn hadn't been stressed about it. But now? *Whoa.*

"Can you talk to Cayden about it over the weekend and get back to me on Monday?" Autumn asked, biting her tongue in order to hold back her frustrations. She understood the complexity of wanting everything just right for a wedding. Heck, she was the wedding planner. Who, of all the people involved in the wedding, wanted things to be one hundred percent flawless. But, wedding colors? That was the easiest choice to make. She couldn't believe it was taking Rylee this long to decide.

Biting her tongue once more, she slid out of the booth after Rylee agreed to let her know the colors come Monday morning at their next coffee talk. Autumn stretched and glanced at the time. She had forgotten to send a text to Charlie to ask if he would like to meet up at the deli across the street for lunch. It wasn't quite lunch time yet, but if she didn't get her things and head out of the coffee shop, she would more than likely say something she would later regret.

"Grab some more coffee and have a seat, Autumn," Fran said, patting the wooden seat beside her. "I want you to tell us about last night."

Autumn looked at Cara, who smiled in return, almost as if she were encouraging Autumn to do what Fran had asked her to. She glanced at Rylee, who was now preparing to leave, and for a second she wanted to apologize to the poor girl who was taking the brunt of Autumn's frustrations. She liked Rylee, and she really didn't have an issue with her.

"Come on," Fran said, reaching for her hand to have her sit down. "I want to hear it from you, the one who experienced it firsthand."

Autumn laughed as she shook her head. "Of course you do," she said, looking back over her shoulder in the direction of the coffee pots. Glancing down at Fran, she said, "Okay, let me go to the restroom and grab some coffee on my way back."

"Sounds good to me," Fran said, leaning back in the booth as she crossed her arms. As Autumn walked away, she heard Fran tell the others, "I have a good feelin' about those two, and I can't wait until they fall in love."

Autumn smiled on her way to the restroom. She would make it quick in order to get back to the one conversation she'd been dying to have. The wedding planning stuff could wait. Something she would have never imagined telling herself, not in a million years. She had once been strictly business, making no time for anything else. Not even her favorite reruns of *I Love Lucy*. But there had been something that changed when she moved to Maple Glen. When she'd reconnected with Charlie.

Charlie. She couldn't wait to see him again. She needed to send him a message and ask if he'd be willing to meet up for lunch. She wanted to see him before he left on his fishing trip with the guys and make sure he didn't feel guilty for leaving her with Cara. Also, she wanted him to know that she wasn't sure how much longer she could stay his friend.

After last night, actually the whole week, she was becoming a different person. She was falling head over heels in love with Charlie Mitchell, and there wasn't a single thing she, or anyone else for that matter, could do to stop the inevitable.

And that was more than okay. She was perfectly fine with falling in love with Charlie as long as he felt the same way about her... A thought hit her hard as she stared at her reflection in the mirror. What if Charlie didn't want to fall in love with her? What if he wasn't willing to be more than just friends? That had been his idea from the beginning, right? What if he never changed his mind?

She brushed a strand of hair behind her ear and pulled open the bathroom door. She didn't have time to think about the *what ifs*. She didn't want to think of what would happen if Charlie refused to fall in love with her. Could a person refuse to fall in love with someone? Was that even possible?

She'd tried several times not to catch feelings, but somehow there she was, falling faster and faster for the one guy who'd vowed to stay *just friends* with.

Refilling her coffee on the way back to the booth, she was

surprised to see it was only Cara and Fran waiting for her to return.

"Rylee and Emmalee had to take off," Fran said, patting the seat next to her. "They had a few things to get done, but Emmalee said they've got a tasty special of the day over at the deli for lunch today."

"Noted," Autumn said with a smile, knowing what Fran was hinting at. It was written all over the woman's face in her cheeky grin as she nodded at Cara. Cara smiled as she looked down at her phone, making it obvious she was avoiding Autumn. "Anyway," Autumn said, pulling their attention back to her. "I think we need to go back to having coffee talk with the girls instead of allowing other distractions to get in the way."

"Distractions?" Fran asked with a grin. "And what would those distractions be that you're speakin' of?"

Autumn chuckled, stacking her notebooks and planners into a neat pile before shoving them into her bag. "I mean, like work stuff and other things that we used to not talk about until after our coffee time was over."

Cara set her phone down and nodded. "I agree. I don't know why we veered away from actually enjoying our coffee in the mornings, but we definitely need to get back to it. Don't you agree, Fran?"

"Well, I most certainly do," Fran said, a wide smile on her face. "But why the change all of a sudden?"

Autumn looked to Cara, who nodded in understanding. It had become so obvious over the last few days that the stress of the wedding planning was taking a toll. She hadn't thought about being stressed doing a job she once enjoyed, but since moving to Maple Glen and having a chance to slow down and enjoy *other* things, Autumn knew better now.

"I just miss it, is all," Autumn said, smiling at Fran.

"There's no sense in coming into the coffee shop in the morning and getting to work right away. We need to relax and enjoy our time together. I mean, we only have so long before Cara marries Vince and we don't see her. Or Emmalee and Clayton with the same chance of never seeing them. You know, because wedded bliss and the honeymoon phase and all," Autumn said, "it's bound to happen at any time now."

"Oh, cut it out," Cara said. "It's not *that* bad."

"Maybe not for you," Autumn said, "but for us it will be."

"Then get to it," Fran said, lightly nudging Autumn with a chuckle. "And, speaking of which, I'm still waitin' to hear all about last night."

Autumn glanced at Cara, who was now too busy texting to chime in. "Okay, but first, let me send an important message."

She grabbed her phone and typed a sweet, inviting message to Charlie. She wanted to see him again. The few minutes she was able to see him this morning while he sat with Fran at the counter hadn't been enough. She wanted to *really* see him. She wanted to have lunch with him. Just the two of them. They could talk and continue on with whatever it was they had going between them while Autumn hoped for the best.

"There," Autumn said, setting her phone down in front of her only to pick it up not even a minute later when it dinged with a notification of an incoming message.

"That was fast," Fran said, taking a drink of coffee and trying her hardest to keep her eyes off Autumn's phone. "Hot date?"

Autumn laughed as she read Charlie's message. Ignoring Fran's question, she said, "I've got a few minutes, so where would you like me to begin?"

"Start from the beginnin'," Fran insisted as she drank her coffee.

Autumn nodded and started from the beginning of their night and ending with Cara arriving because Charlie wanted to make sure she was okay throughout the night.

"Sounds like a real *Prince Charmin'*," Fran said, smiling ear to ear as Autumn slid out of her seat and stood beside the table. "He sounds like he just might be a keeper?"

Autumn couldn't agree more. The way they'd sang together on stage and how well they'd performed a few of her favorite country songs… "I think you might be right," Autumn said, daydreaming of the man who stole her heart the first time she'd met him and refusing to give it back to her. That was more than okay. He could keep it as long as he didn't break it.

CHAPTER FOURTEEN

Seeing the text from Autumn, he couldn't help but smile. He'd been packing and preparing to head out on the trip.

I'll meet you there in ten minutes.

He typed the message back and hit send, hoping ten minutes wouldn't be rushing her away from coffee with the girls.

His phone vibrated in his pocket not even two minutes later, and he couldn't believe what she'd sent. He had to read it again.

Ok. Can't wait to see you.

He traced his thumb across the letters of his phone's keyboard, hitting the delete button several times before he was happy with what he wrote.

Neither can I ;)

Smiling and wishing he could see her reaction when she read the message, he hit send.

The winky face was what he figured would do her in. He knew that him admitting he couldn't wait to see her wouldn't have nearly enough effect on her as the winky face.

His phone vibrated against his hand, causing him to unlock it in order to hurry up and read her message.

;)

He couldn't help but smile. "So long, heart," he whispered to no one but himself. He was standing alone in the middle of his kitchen getting ready to leave.

Grabbing his truck keys, he tucked his phone in his pocket and headed out the door. He couldn't wait to see her and make sure she wasn't upset at him for leaving her like he had.

If the smile on her face from this morning, and the messages just now, were to be taken as a sign, he'd say he was safe and she was far from upset.

Turning the key in the ignition, he fired up his old truck and pulled out of the driveway.

He'd be at the deli in less than five minutes, which gave him plenty of time to think about what he'd say to her.

After spending the time they'd had together last night, and after leaving her in the care of his sister, it became obvious how much he cared about her... which was more than just friends.

He'd wanted to kiss her and wrap his arms around her, pulling her close to him as he told her how happy she made him.

That thought alone made him happy. He couldn't continue on with acting like he wasn't crazy about her when it was the complete opposite. He couldn't stop thinking about her and how happy she made him when they were together. It was something he'd waited so long to find, and he'd finally found it. Right here in Maple Glen.

Pulling into a vacant spot out front of his brother's business, he killed the engine and hopped out of his truck. He glanced inside the large open windows as he headed for the door. He swore his heart skipped a beat and he missed a step when his eyes landed on her.

Sitting in a booth all by herself, with long curls covering her bare shoulders and those kissable lips that matched the color of the sweetest wine, Autumn was everything he needed in his life, and he couldn't wait another minute to tell her exactly how he felt about her while saying a silent prayer that she felt the same way about him.

Pushing through the door, the bell announced his arrival, and no sooner than he stepped one foot in the direction of Autumn's booth, Clayton called out from the back of the deli, "Charlie, we need to talk."

When Charlie looked to Autumn and back to Clayton, he narrowed his eyes and motioned to his brother that there was something more important to tend to, but the look on his brother's face trumped his own. A look of worry and anguish lined his face.

"Now," Clayton said, not giving Charlie a choice but to leave Autumn waiting a few more minutes.

Autumn offered an understanding look as she motioned for him to go ahead and talk to his brother. As he walked past her, he said, "This won't take but a minute or two."

"Okay," she said, smiling as though she were anticipating his return.

On his way past the kitchen area, he waved at Emmalee, who smiled and returned a friendly wave. He wondered if Autumn had told her anything about what was happening between them. Smiling, he approached his brother, "What's so important that it can't wait until after—"

"It's Dad," Clayton said, grabbing hold of Charlie's sleeve and pulling him into the back room which led to the meat locker portion of the business. Charlie ripped his sleeve out of Clayton's grasp. "What about him? What's goin' on?"

He could tell by the panic in his brother's voice and the way he couldn't stand still, there was something not right. Clayton paced around the back room, running a hand through his hair. Charlie grabbed hold of his arm and jerked to get him to stop and focus. "What's goin' on? Is he alright?"

"I don't think Mom was supposed to tell me," Clayton said, gripping the back of his neck as he leaned against the wall. "I think it just came out before she had a chance to realize she'd said too much."

"That doesn't seem to be your problem right now. If you don't spit it out I swear I'm gonna—"

"Dad has cancer."

The words punched him straight in his stomach. Gut checked and barely breathing, Charlie leaned against the doorjamb. "It can't be. They've told him that once before and they were wrong," Charlie said, running an unsteady hand through his hair. He couldn't imagine life without his father. Sure, his parents were living in Florida and enjoying the sun's rays on the many beaches down there, and they hardly saw them, but still... "I mean, the tests... they could have it all wrong again like last time, right?"

Clayton shook his head, allowing Charlie to face reality before it slapped him. "Not this time. They've run several tests over the last week, and they're convinced he's got—"

"No," Charlie said, pushing off the doorjamb and walking toward the table in the center of the room. "Don't even say it."

"I don't think Mom was supposed to tell me," Clayton said, adding fuel to the fire Charlie felt burning in his gut. He quirked a brow in Clayton's direction, willing him to explain what the heck he was even talking about. "I think Dad wanted to keep a secret from us kids, and Mom wasn't supposed to tell me, but she did."

"Obviously."

Charlie knew better than to get smart with Clayton, but there was no time for captain obvious. They needed to figure out what this meant for their father. What it meant for their family. For their mother.

The thought of losing his father... he couldn't imagine life without him in it.

"Don't even start with me," Clayton said, pointing a finger in Charlie's face. Charlie shoved it away and grabbed a chair so he could sit down. He couldn't believe anything he'd heard.

"Cancer?" Charlie's question came out in a squeak, his voice full of emotion. "What? What kind are we talkin' about?"

Clayton shook his head and said, "I'm not exactly sure, but it doesn't sound good. Mom said the doctor isn't givin' him long to live."

Charlie stood from his chair, slamming it back with his legs. "Son of a—"

"Hey," Clayton shouted, rising from his own chair and grabbing hold of Charlie. There was no sense in Clayton trying to calm him down. His emotions were all over the place, and the only true emotion he felt that very minute was complete anger and denial. He refused to believe his father would die according to the doctor's schedule. What kind of doctor announces a time frame to a patient who was just told they had cancer? "We've gotta do what we can to stay calm. If not for ourselves and each other, for Mom."

Charlie nodded as tears stung his eyes and blurred his vision. He hated crying. Hated it with a passion, but right now, he couldn't care less. He needed to talk to his father. He needed to tell him that he loved him. "Yeah, you're right," Charlie said, reaching into his pocket and digging his phone out. He stared at a blank screen, wondering why their mother hadn't called him. Maybe Clayton was right. Maybe she didn't mean to let it slip. But now the cat was out of the bag, and Charlie couldn't stop his mind from racing in all directions. Thinking of the *what ifs* and wondering if there was a chance the tests were wrong, even if Clayton said there wasn't. "Should we call a family meeting? Tell the others all at the same time?"

Clayton shrugged his shoulders, making it obvious he hadn't thought too far ahead of where they were standing at now. The girls were in the deli laughing, and as bad as Charlie wanted to open the door and yell at them for being insensitive and obnoxious, he knew they had no idea what was going on between him and Clayton. They were carrying on their own conversation and entertaining each other.

Shaking his head, ignoring the distraction happening out front, Charlie said, "What do we do? Are they coming back to Maple Glen for treatments? So he can see his regular doctor?"

Clayton shook his head again, and if Charlie didn't know any better, he'd think the man didn't know a damn thing. Frustration coursed through Charlie's veins, seeping into his concentration and inability to stay focused on the here and now. He needed to know what to do next. Standing around and talking about it wasn't going to help their father. But what could? "Is he gonna do chemotherapy or whatever the heck it's called?"

Clayton pinched the bridge of his nose and let out a heavy groan. "I don't know what he's going to do because Mom didn't say. She wasn't even wantin' to tell me about it in the first place," he said, dropping his hand from his face and staring Charlie directly in the eyes. "I don't know what we should do, or what we shouldn't do. Everything's a damn blur, and I can't even think straight."

Charlie nodded, knowing exactly how his brother felt because he was right there with him. They were on the rollercoaster from hell together, and as far as Charlie could tell, there was no way to jump off of it this time.

"We should tell the others," Charlie insisted, tapping his knuckles on the countertop. "They need to know what's goin' on, and once they know, we can come up with a plan—"

"A plan? For what? You think we'll be able to cure his cancer?"

Charlie took a step back and stared at his brother like he'd lost his mind. "Are you serious right now?"

"Are you? Can you even hear what you're sayin'?"

"You know what? I don't need this," Charlie said, turning in the direction of the door and preparing himself to leave his brother standing alone in the meat locker. "You think you've got all the answers, but you don't. You're just wanting to stand around and talk about it. Like that's gonna help our dad. Mock me all you want, but at least I'll be doin' somethin' about it."

Before he had a chance to close the door behind him, Clayton grabbed his arm and pulled him back. "Wait," he said, making Charlie face him. "I'm sorry, I just. I don't know what to do. I'm the oldest, and I feel like I should know what to do... what to say... and I don't... at all."

Defeat crossed his brother's face, and Charlie felt it, too. "We've gotta call the others and let them know," Charlie said, reaching for his phone once again. This time, he was going to dial his siblings' phone numbers and tell them the news about their father. "But first, I need to tell Autumn what's goin' on so she knows."

Clayton nodded and followed him through the door and

into the deli. The girls were sitting in the booth across from one another, still laughing and having a good time. More than likely they were sharing stories of dates, and he wouldn't put it past Emmalee to be asking all kinds of questions while trying to figure out the status between Charlie and Autumn. He shook his head. What had seemed like a big deal yesterday—figuring out how to move out of the friend zone to something more promising—wasn't anywhere close to the big deal he was facing now.

"Hey you guys," Emmalee greeted them as they walked past the kitchen area and toward their booth. "About time you come out of hiding."

Looking at Charlie, Emmalee said, "You shouldn't keep a girl waiting, you know? If it wasn't for me, Autumn would be sitting all alone and bored out of her mind."

Her voice was chipper, but he could hear the *tsk tsk* as she scowled at him.

"Em, now's not the time," Clayton said, motioning for her to scoot over and allow him to sit down beside her. Charlie followed suit and did the same with Autumn, who was already scooting over before he made it obvious he wanted to sit down. "We've got some things to figure out and wanted to let you guys know before we tell everyone else."

Charlie caught Autumn staring at him from the corner of his eye. She was looking to him for answers—an explanation—but he didn't have the right words to say what needed to be said.

"What's going on?" Emmalee said, looking back and forth between Clayton and Charlie. "What's this about? Does it have to deal with the phone call—"

"Yes," Clayton said, reaching for her hand and holding it. "Dad's got cancer, and the doctor in Florida says he doesn't have long to live."

Clayton's words came out in a rush, filled with emotion but cold as ice. Charlie knew he wouldn't have been able to say it any better, and definitely not as calmly. Autumn's hand reached out and grabbed his. He looked over and her soft blue eyes were filled with concern. The warmth of her hand surpassed the numbness he felt and went straight to his heart. Offering a sympathetic smile, she squeezed his hand and said, "I'm sorry, Char. Just let me know what you need, and I'll do whatever I can to help."

Emmalee nodded, reassuring Clayton with the same words and loving support. Charlie looked at Clayton, wondering if he'd known Emmalee was the one for him when he'd first met her, but quickly dismissed those thoughts when he remembered his brother telling him that he wasn't too happy about Emmalee's invitation from their parents to work at the deli.

"Thank you," he said, turning his attention back to Autumn, who now had tears in her eyes. She tried to keep them from falling, he could tell by the pressed line of her lips and her inability to talk. She nodded and they escaped, one trailing gently behind the other down her cheek. "Hey, it's okay. Don't cry."

She shook her head with a half laugh as she quickly wiped them away with the sleeve of her shirt. "Gah, I'm so emotional," she said, chastising herself for crying. "Here I am bawling like a baby and it's not even—"

"No," he said, pulling her close to him as he wrapped his arm around her. "Don't. It's okay."

Emmalee handed a few napkins across the table and used one to dab at her own watery eyes. Clayton hugged her close to his chest as he looked over at Charlie. Charlie could see right through him. Despite being the older of the two, Clayton was at a loss for words, and Charlie could tell he had no idea what to do or where to go next.

A part of Charlie wanted to pack up and head to Florida. Instead of taking the fishing trip they'd planned to take, they could take the trip to Florida. "What do you think they'd do if we showed up at their house?"

"I guess there's only one way to find out," Clayton said, pulling his phone out of the front pocket of his jeans and typing something into the search bar on his screen. "Looks like the next available flight out there is in two days."

Clayton flipped his phone around, showing Charlie the screen filled with options for taking a plane to Florida. "Looks like we're goin' to Florida," he said, tapping on his brother's number on his phone before lifting it to his ear. Clayton nodded and tapped an option as Charlie waited for Cayden to answer. He didn't want to be the bearer of bad news, but someone had to do it. Clayton was busy booking their flights, and Charlie needed to do something without feeling helpless.

"Hey, man, what's up?" Cayden answered after the second ring. "I just got back from Carter's. We went out to the ledge and caught a few—"

"Cayden, listen," Charlie said, his tone coming out a bit too harsh. "Somethin's come up, and we need you to meet us at the deli."

"What?" Cayden's tone dropped from upbeat and ecstatic to panic ridden. "What's goin' on? Is Clayton okay? Emma—"

"They're fine, but you need to get here," Charlie said, trying his best to keep his temper in check. "I gotta call the others. I'll see you in a bit?"

"Yeah, of course," Cayden said, the sound of shuffling in the background. "I'll be right there."

Charlie hung up the phone and, before he called the others, he looked at Clayton and said, "I'm not sure how Cayden's going to take the news. I mean, his wedding is, what? A few weeks away, if that?"

"Yeah," Autumn said, looking down at her books in front of her. "Three weeks and two days, to be exact."

The thought of their father not surviving long enough to see Cayden's wedding, or anyone else's for that matter, was enough to crush Charlie. Not to mention that Cayden was the baby of the family... It just didn't seem right. It wasn't fair. There was no way they were going to let their father die. They needed to make sure he didn't give up. He needed to fight, and there was no way Charlie was going to allow cancer to take his father away from them.

CHAPTER FIFTEEN

*C*ancer. The word itself was daunting, and the meaning behind it brought nightmarish images from her past. The pain of hearing the news made her heart break, and thoughts of losing her grandfather to cancer resurfaced, making it impossible to keep her emotions in check. Empathy ran deep within Autumn. She lived her whole life supporting others and helping them through their troubled times, but nothing quite like this. Cancer had taken its toll on her own family a few years ago, and Cara had helped her through it. It was time to return the favor.

Autumn's attempt to be strong for Charlie failed as he sat beside her, making phone calls in order to round up everyone for an emergency family meeting. She had thought about leaving the deli, but she felt like she should stick around for not only Charlie, but Cara, too. Cara would need her through this, and even if Charlie and Autumn weren't an *official* couple *yet*, there was a chance that Charlie would need her just as much, if not more.

. . .

"Cara's on her way," Charlie said, aiming his words at Autumn more than anyone else. Autumn nodded, knowing what it meant and what she would have to do. It was time to step up and be the rock her best friend was going to need. "She's already thinkin' the worst case—"

The bell above the door announced Cara's arrival before they heard her voice. "What's goin' on?"

A look of panic flashed across Cara's face as she rounded the corner, seeking out the booth currently occupied by some of her family. She sought Autumn out of the crowd and quirked her brow, silently pleading for answers to her unspoken questions. Autumn motioned for Cara to come around the booth and sit down beside her and she obliged, thankfully. She hated to see her best friend so worried, and she wanted to be right there when she needed a shoulder to cry on. They could cry together.

Autumn didn't know Scott too well, but from the time or two she'd talked with him, he was a pretty great guy. He had a sharp wit and a sense of humor, and he was always up for a challenging debate. Honestly, he reminded Autumn of her grandfather. The only differing factor between them was their age.

"Do you know what's going on?" Cara whispered as she leaned into Autumn's side. Autumn pressed her lips together, holding back from telling her and allowing Clayton or Charlie to instead. "Okay, then," Cara said, straightening and crossing her arms over her chest. "Will someone please tell me what in the heck is going on?"

Autumn glanced across the table at Clayton, who turned his eyes on Charlie. Charlie swallowed hard and wrung his hands in front of him. Autumn relaxed her hand on his forearm after realizing she had been gripping it for the last few minutes while sitting among them, silently praying that they'd be okay.

"We have to wait for Carter and Cayden to get here," Charlie said, his voice edged with frustration and his jaw tense. "Cassie and Catie are on their way, too."

Cara glared at Clayton but remained silent. If looks could kill, her brother would be dead. Emmalee shot a look in Cara's direction, offering what appeared to be a sympathetic frown. Autumn assumed from the looks of it, Emmalee was awkward and more than likely not used to death. Death must not have ever wreaked havoc in her life, or threatened to take the people she loved the most. Autumn knew better than to judge her for it, but envied her if that was the case.

She would have loved to know what it was like without seeing death firsthand. She wanted to know what it was like to have a grandfather to take his granddaughter fishing when her father was too busy at work to spend more than ten minutes a day with her.

"Autumn…" Cara whispered, gripping Autumn's hand while silently pleading her to say something, anything.

Autumn shook her head, not wanting to be the one to tell her. She needed to hear it from her brothers. They were the ones who needed to tell her, to tell them—the rest of the Mitchell family—about Scott. "Care, I—"

A heavy sigh escaped her lips as she tossed her head back. Tears shined in her eyes, making it obvious that even though she hadn't the slightest idea about what was going on, deep down Cara already knew it wasn't good. "I just need to know what's going on."

The bell above the door announced another arrival. Three more people, who Autumn assumed to be Carter, Cayden, and one of the sisters, stood by their table expressing the same concerns that Cara had.

Charlie looked up at them, still not ready to share the news about their father until the last sibling showed up.

"Cassie, have you seen Catie? I thought you two were workin' on the bed and breakfast together," Clayton said, sliding out of the booth and making his way to an unoccupied table. He grabbed two long tables and slid them together, making more room for his family to sit down and talk. Motioning for his family to move to the table, Clayton said, "Let's sit over here instead."

The family moved in silent unison. No one said a word, but Autumn knew what they were all thinking. It was written on their faces. The worst was yet to come.

Taking a seat by Cara, not paying attention to where Charlie had decided to sit, Autumn felt his eyes on her from the end of the table. When she met his eyes with hers, her heart demanded to be released from her chest as it pounded against her ribs. The effect he had on her was unlike anything she'd ever experienced except when she was around him, and certainly this wasn't the time to allow him to affect her like that. She needed to pull it together.

Turning to Cara, she said, "I just want you to know that I'm here for you. Whatever you need, just know I'm here."

When Cara looked at her, she didn't say a word. Instead, she looked puzzled, almost distraught as though the thoughts inside her head were too much for her to think straight. To comprehend what Autumn was trying so hard to tell her.

"Okay?" Autumn squeezed Cara's hand, forcing back the tears that threatened to stream freely down her cheeks at any given moment.

Cara opened her mouth to say something but closed it as she nodded. "Okay."

Autumn felt the weight of the world on her shoulders while keeping the news from Cara. She wanted nothing more than to tell her. To tell her and make sure she knew that Autumn was there with her, for her. For them. Autumn wouldn't stray. She would stand by and make sure they were okay, no matter what happened.

After waiting for what felt like an eternity, the bell sang its last announcement and Catie appeared at the end of the table next to Charlie and Clayton. "What's goin' on, and why do I get a sense this isn't good," she said, staring around the room as her eyes landed on each and every person seated around the table.

"Because it's not," Clayton said, scooting his chair out away from the table and offering her to take his seat, but she refused, finding her own next to Carter. Clayton looked at Charlie, and Autumn could see the hesitation in his eyes, the tension set in his jawline. He was not ready to tell his family the news about their father. Charlie glanced up and, still keeping his hands folded in front of him, he said, "Just tell them already. We've waited long enough."

Clayton looked down at his hands and back up at his family. Clearing his throat and offering a nervous grunt, he said, "There's really no easy way to say this, so I'm just going to say it."

Everyone sitting around the table looked at each other and back at Clayton, ready to hear what he had to say. "What's goin' on?" Carter asked, agitation deep in his voice as his eyes focused on Clayton.

"Dad has cancer," Clayton said, allowing the words to fall out of his mouth and attempting to maintain composure as he stammered over his next bout of words, "and the doctor's not givin' him long to live."

The Mitchell sisters gasped, pulling each other close and crying out indecipherable words as they clung to one another. Autumn hung on to Cara, allowing her to cry against her as the uncontrollable sobs wracked through her body. "I'm so sorry, Care Bear," she whispered, combing her fingers through her best friend's hair and wishing to take away the uncertainty of tomorrow for them. "Your dad's strong. He'll make it through this, I just know it."

The words she spoke, although sincere and full of hope, fell flat and unbelievable. She knew what cancer could do. She had seen cancer rip her family apart and gave them no chance to hope for the best before taking the rock of their family away from them and out of this world.

"How long are they givin' him to live?" Cayden's question silenced the room. The sisters hung close together, embracing one another and looking at Cayden like he—not the cancer—was the monster that was trying to take their father away from them.

"Cayden—"

He held up a hand and silenced Cara from saying anything else. "Answer the question, Clay," he demanded, staring his brother down from across the table.

Clayton shrugged, clearing his throat of the emotion threatening to choke him. "I don't know. Mom didn't say," he explained, keeping his voice low and his eyes focused on his hands in front of him. "I don't think they wanted us to know."

"What? You're kidding, right?" Carter said, shoving his chair back as he stood from the table. "How could they not want us to know? Wouldn't we be the first to know?"

Autumn watched as he paced the floor, running a stressed hand through his hair over and over again. Everyone handled the news differently, but from the looks of it they were taking it a heck of a lot better than Autumn had thought they would. Unlike when she had first heard the news of her grandfather's cancer… She had been too emotional and out of her mind to be consoled.

"Maybe Dad didn't want us to worry," Clayton said, trying his best to explain something Autumn knew he wasn't even sure about himself.

"Yeah, that's great," Carter said, sitting back down in his abandoned chair. "What do you suppose we should do now that we *do* know?"

Clayton glanced around the room, and Autumn waited with bated breath, hoping someone would say something to ease the tension before it burst. She looked at Charlie, willing him to say something, anything, to get the tension to dissipate. He was used to breaking up tense situations, wasn't he? He owned a bar for Pete's sake.

He caught her looking at him, but instead of looking away, he held her stare for a minute longer before he said, "Instead of taking the fishin' trip, we go to Florida instead."

The two younger brothers groaned but quickly shaped up when they caught the glares from their older brothers. The sisters glanced at each other and back to Clayton. Autumn felt as though she were in a movie, acting a part of an extra and remaining quiet as the family sorted everything out around her. She was there for support—for both Cara and Charlie. She glanced across the table at Emmalee, who was in the same boat as her. Uncertain about what to do or say other than to sit quietly and wait for the storm to pass.

Except the storm wasn't going to pass. At least not for quite some time.

"What about my wedding?" Cayden asked, garnering him negative reactions from all around him. He held up his hands, trying his best to ward off the insults his question had unleashed.

Cara slammed her hand on the table and Autumn held on tight to her arm, preparing to hold her back from attacking her brother. "How can you be so selfish and uncaring? Who cares about your wedding when Dad's dying!"

Carter slammed his fist on the table, knocking the chair over as he stood. "Enough!"

The room silenced once again. Autumn held her breath, willing for the confrontation and arguing to stop.

"Dad's not dyin'," Carter said, bound and determined to make them believe him. "Your wedding is the last thing we need to worry about."

Autumn knew by the tone in Carter's voice that he was at his breaking point. No matter how hard he tried to hide it, she could tell. She glanced at Charlie, who caught her staring and looked away, and she knew that he was just as troubled by the news as the others were, if not more.

"Easy for you to say when you're not the one gettin' married, jack—"

"Enough," Charlie said, raising his voice but reining in his anger unlike his brothers. "We'll figure this out, but first, we need to head to Florida and see what's goin' on with our own eyes. Until our flights are booked and we've landed in Florida, there will be no slammin' each other and blowin' things out of proportion. I don't care who's gettin' married and who isn't. It's not about us. Got it?"

Silent nods answered him. "Good. Then this meeting is over," he announced, standing from his chair. "Clayton and I will book our flights and let you know when we're leavin'. For now, we wait and hope Mom keeps us updated."

His eyes landed on her, and a breath hitched in her throat. She was trying so hard to remain quiet and strong for those who needed her. Trying just as hard to keep herself together as emotions roared through her.

"Let's go," Charlie said, motioning for her to follow him out the door.

She turned to Cara and offered her one last hug. She wanted to stay and comfort her best friend, but she also wanted to be by Charlie's side as well. Cara must have sensed it, because she said, "Go ahead, I'll be fine. Please make sure he doesn't do anything stupid."

Autumn smiled and pulled away as she looked her in the eye. "I can't make any promises, but I'll do my best."

Cara cracked a smile and pulled Autumn close for one more hug before allowing her to leave. "I love you, Autumn."

"I love you, too, Care Bear," Autumn called over her shoulder. Walking out the door, she couldn't help but wonder what Charlie had in mind. She would go wherever he wanted her to go, but if he needed time alone, she would be more than willing to give him space. She just wanted to make sure he was going to be okay.

CHAPTER SIXTEEN

"Shouldn't we stay with your family?" Autumn asked, making her way toward him as he leaned against the bed of his truck.

He kept his eyes on her as she approached him. She looked beyond incredible today, much like any other day, except today she'd tugged at his emotional side and held on tight when he needed it the most. He wouldn't be the one to tell her how scared he was to lose his father.

Heck, by the look on her face and the knowing glances she was giving him, she already knew.

His emotions were his weakness. He would like to think he was a strong man who could withstand all that life threw at him, but *this*... his father dying a slow and agonizing death while his kids gathered at his bedside... That thought alone was too much to bear, and he knew if it weren't for Autumn's gentle grasp and her soft spoken words, he would have lost it in front of everyone inside.

"They'll be fine," he said, clearing his throat and pushing off the side of his truck. "I had to get out of there or else I would've done somethin' I'd regret later."

She quirked a brow and leaned against his truck. "And what's that?"

He shrugged and rested his arms back on the bedliner as he leaned in. She was directly across from him, giving him a challenging look that made him want to take her face in his hands and kiss those wine-colored lips of hers. He shook his head. His thoughts were going to get him in trouble. He wasn't even sure where they stood. The only thing he knew for sure was that where they were now was a lot further along than the place they'd been. They'd been toeing the line between friends and something more while daring one another to be the one to cross it.

"Charlie?" She was beside him now, reaching out and touching his arm, sending a thousand volts of electricity from her fingertips. "What can I do to help? I want—"

In that moment, he could no longer hold back the urge raging through him. The current she'd sent forth zapped through his body, causing an inability to think only to act. Gently but firmly he grabbed her face and pressed his lips to hers.

Startled, she leaned back at first only to lean into him and kiss him with the same need that left them both hungry for more.

She stepped back, pulling away from him as she looked into his eyes. "What if you regret this?"

He shook his head. She thought he was acting on impulse. Acting out of his inability to control his emotions and what's happening with his father. "I won't... I don't. Not a chance."

She looked up at him with doubt clearly written on her face. "What were you going to do in there that you would've regretted later, then?"

"That has nothin' to do with *us... this...*"

He couldn't help but pull her close to him, wrapping his

arms around her as he looked into her eyes. He had so much he wanted to say but didn't have the right words to say it.

"What is *this*, exactly?"

"Autumn, I..."

"Get a room!" His brother, Carter, hollered from the sidewalk in front of the deli. "We don't wanna see that!"

"Mind your own business!" he hollered back, flipping his brother the bird behind Autumn's back.

Carter shook his head and continued walking in the direction of his car. "When you're done playin' tonsil hockey—"

His glare cut him off. Carter held up his hands. "Alright, I'm outta here."

Autumn laughed against his chest, and the sound was everything he needed to hear. The next few days were going to be nothing but crazy and tense as they figured out what was going on with his father.

"How was it, growing up with him?" she asked, hooking a thumb in Carter's direction as he pulled out of his parking spot and drove past them. "Because I have a feeling it wasn't easy."

Charlie tipped his head back laughing. "Nothin's ever easy when it comes to havin' siblings, right?"

She shrugged a shoulder as she pulled away from him. "I don't know. My brother died when we were little."

He looked down at the ground, at the painted line next to his back tire. "I'm sorry," he said, feeling like a heel for not knowing. "I had no idea."

"It's okay," she said, waving off his apology like it was no big deal. "I don't even think Cara knows. And she knows *everything*."

"*Everything*?" He couldn't help wondering if she'd mentioned anything about them and recent events to his sister.

She nodded while giving him a sly smile. "Every. Single. Thing."

He smiled, knowing he was in for it when it came to Cara if things didn't work out. Not that he wanted things to go downhill because he'd had enough of that crap. He wanted something good for a change. Something he wouldn't allow his fears or insecurities to take away and ruin for him. Autumn was the one he wanted to spend his time with. When he looked at his brothers—in love and falling head over heels for their women—he craved what they had. There wasn't anything else he wanted so badly in all of his years alive except to find a woman to share the rest of his life with.

And the one he wanted was standing in front of him.

"Then I guess I should make sure whatever *this* is between us ends on a good note?"

She playfully slapped his arm. "Ends? You're already thinking about it ending?"

He'd said it as a tease, a way to get her to laugh and carry on like two fools in love, but what he got was a head full of insecure thoughts in response to her question.

"Is that a yes?" she asked, pulling him from his thoughts.

"What? No," he said, "not at all. That's the furthest thing from what I want. It's just…"

He couldn't finish his sentence. He couldn't tell her how he felt, or she'd know how insecure he was. How weak he was. It didn't take a genius to know women don't like sensitive men. They want strong, capable men who are able to face anything and keep their emotions hidden from the world.

"Just what?"

He shook his head, wanting her to forget he'd said anything. "It's nothin'."

"Is this not what you want? Are you having doubts already?" She offered a slight nudge to the crook of his arm and chuckled. "You don't have to look so worried. It's not like we're getting married tomorrow."

She meant it as a joke, but he couldn't help but wonder... "Would you, though? Would you marry me?"

Her eyes widened as she stepped back, looking at him like he'd lost his mind. Maybe he had. Maybe he shouldn't have asked her like that. It wasn't like he was actually proposing...

"Whoa," she said, tucking a strand of loose hair behind her ear before turning back to face him. "Are you—"

"Relax, I was just askin' out of curiosity," he said, holding his hands up to protect himself if she decided to lash out at him for being an idiot. He wouldn't blame her if she did. He probably shouldn't have asked at all. "Unless, of course, you want—"

"Stop right there," she said, shaking her head. "Let's get through one thing at a time. Right now, we need to... well, *I* need to finish planning Cayden and Rylee's wedding. And then we can talk."

He laughed, refusing to believe for a second she was serious about tabling this conversation for a later time. Marriage would come sooner or later without having to rush it.

Then it hit him. Cayden's wedding. His father's prognosis.

Time wasn't guaranteed, and it was only a matter of time before he lost his father.

CHAPTER SEVENTEEN

A knock at the door pulled her attention away from watching *I Love Lucy*. Checking the time on her phone and realizing she had spent the last two hours fully engrossed in the show, she made her way to the door.

It had been a long, emotional day, and to see Charlie through the peephole, standing right outside her door, caused her heart to skip a few beats. Unlocking the door, she opened it in one swift motion and smiled. "What are you doing here?"

His smile displayed the dimples that she loved the most and his familiar smell instantly eased some of her exhaustion. "Is that how you always answer the door?"

"It is when it's after nine at night and you interrupted my show," she said, motioning for him to come inside. Shutting the door behind him, she offered to take his jacket, hoping he was planning to stay for more than a few minutes.

"And what show were you watching?"

His question was innocent enough, but she still debated on telling him just for the sake of being made fun of. Not too many women her age lived for watching *I Love Lucy* reruns every night after work while eating ice cream—alone.

"I'll tell you if you promise not to laugh at me," she said, jumping in front of the television so he wouldn't be able to see the paused image on the screen.

He chuckled as he walked to the couch and sat down. "I won't laugh."

She raised a brow while placing a hand on her hip. "Promise?"

A grunt sounded in the base of his throat before he offered a slight chuckle and said, "I promise."

She adored the way he rolled his eyes in a playful manner as she debated on whether or not to come clean about her addiction to watching reruns of the older shows her mother and grandmother watched when they were younger.

Sighing, she said, "Okay, but only because you promised not to laugh."

She stepped to the side, and once Lucy's face was in full view, Charlie quirked a brow. "*I Love Lucy?*"

"You do?" she asked, maybe just a bit too excited because he laughed in response. Not just a regular laugh, but a full-on, belly-rolling laugh. "Wait…"

"No, I was saying the name of the show," he said, pointing at the screen beside her, proudly displaying Lucy's face mid sentence.

"Go ahead and laugh," she said, rolling her eyes and waiting for the jokes to start.

"Laugh? Why would I?" he asked, patting the couch beside him as he reached for the TV remote and hit play. "I love Lucy."

"No, you don't," she said, making her way around the coffee table to sit down beside him. "It's okay. You don't have to say that to make me feel better."

He shook his head. "No, seriously, aside from the manly shows I watch, I'm okay with watching shows like this every once and awhile."

"Really?"

She was having a hard time believing him, but the look on his face showed no signs of joking.

"Really," he admitted. "And as long as I'm here with you, I wouldn't care if you had me watch the most ridiculous show of all time."

She laughed this time, knowing that there was always an opportunity to make him watch something like that with her, but not right now. Right now, she would enjoy his company and spend the extra time she had with him before he had to leave for Florida.

"I mean it," he said, reaching over and pulling her closer. She scooted closer, closing the gap between them as she sidled up next to him.

"I know," she said, smiling ear to ear because of how cheesy it was.

"I wish I didn't have to leave tomorrow," he whispered, a slight hesitancy in his voice. "I want you to come with me."

"I can't," she said. "I have a wedding to plan, but I would go in a heartbeat if I could."

"I'm kinda afraid to see him tomorrow," he said, and the pain in his words made her feel for him. She wouldn't wish that on her own worst enemy. She could see the glistening of tears in his eyes, reflecting in the light from the television. He leaned back, and she sensed the frustration. "I just don't know—"

"It's okay," she said, trying her best to reassure him. "Just take it one day at a time."

He nodded, letting her know that he agreed and said, "I didn't come here to talk about it, though. I came here to be with you and to spend time with you before I face the hell that's comin'."

"Okay," she said. "What do you have in mind?"

She held her breath, knowing of several things they *could* do to spend their time together, but she'd let him decide the night's events.

He pointed to the television and said, "Have you ever made out while watching *I Love Lucy*?"

"No!" She slapped him in the arm and laughed. "What kind of question is that?"

"I was only jokin'," he said, rubbing the sore spot on his arm. "Dang. Anyway, why don't we just watch your show and see where the night takes us?"

"I like the sound of that," she said, snuggling close to him as he wrapped his arms around her. Pulling her against him, he kissed the top of her head. She tipped her head back and looked him in the eye. He leaned down and pressed his lips against hers, awakening the butterflies once again. She would never tire of the feeling he caused when he kissed her like that.

"You're missing your show," he joked, offering her a wink.

"I don't care about that right now."

She knew they only had a few hours to spend together before he had to leave for Florida, and she would enjoy every minute she had with him. She said a silent prayer for his father while saying one for Charlie, too.

Walking into Fran's Coffee the next morning didn't feel the same as it had in the past.

The worry about Scott Mitchell weighed heavily on

everyone's minds. Fran was chatting with another customer about her brother-in-law being tough and how the big *C* wouldn't keep him down for long. He'd be back on his feet in no time.

Autumn didn't know the extent of his prognosis, but it hadn't sounded good when Clayton had announced it. With the doctor not giving him long to live...

She couldn't think about it. Instead, she thought of sweet treats and coffee. A perfect blend for the morning after all the emotions wreaked havoc on her mind. Who was she kidding? Sweets and coffee could only do so much for her troubled mind.

"Good mornin', dear," Fran greeted as she rounded the counter and headed her way. "Are you havin' your usual this mornin'?"

Autumn glanced at the menu board behind Fran. She wanted something different, but didn't know what to choose. "Surprise me," she said, pulling money from her wallet and setting it on the counter. "Just give it a double shot of espresso, please?"

"You got it, honey," Fran said, carrying on with her day-to-day routine of preparing coffee. Autumn smiled at the thought that Fran could possibly make coffee in her sleep without missing a step. "The girls are gonna be a little late this mornin'. Cara's got somethin' goin' on but won't say what it is, and Emmalee... well, I guess she won't be in today at all because she's on her way to the airport with the rest of the clan."

Autumn saw the expression on Fran's face and asked, "Is everything alright with Cara?"

A smug grin spread across Fran's face. "Well, I sure hope so," she said, placing Autumn's cup of coffee on the counter in front of her. "They say there's a stomach bug goin' around,

CHRISTINA BUTRUM

but I know better than to believe that. There aren't any stomach bugs in September."

Autumn grabbed her coffee and took a drink. The first drink in the morning was always the best. Hands down, the best. And it was an added bonus that it was Fran's coffee.

"So, we're just waitin' on Cara," Fran said, a smile on her face as she pointed in the direction of their booth. "Rylee's been here since the crack of dawn. I'm thinkin' the stress of everything is gettin' to her."

Autumn glanced over at the booth, and sure enough, Rylee was sitting there all alone tracing her finger around the rim of her cup. "Have you heard anything more from Linda?"

Fran set her rag down on the counter and sighed. "No, I haven't. And I'm not sure we're going to."

Autumn took another drink of her coffee before setting it down on the counter. She wanted to sit, but she realized Fran was keeping herself occupied and avoiding the booth. "Why's that?"

Fran shrugged. "Linda didn't want anyone to know. They were going to try and take care of everythin' on their own. It was my idea for her to tell the kids. She didn't even want to tell 'em."

"It's got to be hard on her," Autumn said, thinking about her grandmother when her grandfather was first diagnosed. The hope she'd had that everything would be okay and that he'd get better kept her going most days. It seemed like that was an ongoing theme. No one ever wanted to believe their time was up with someone they loved. "I remember when my grandpa was diagnosed and given a few weeks to live…"

Fran sighed, tossing a dirty rag into the sink behind her. "Oh, dear, I'm so sorry," she said, moving around the counter in Autumn's direction. "Let's go sit down."

Autumn grabbed her coffee and followed Fran to their

booth. Rylee's eyes met hers, and it only took a second to realize the effect the news of Scott's cancer had on her. Autumn wondered what it would mean for Cayden and Rylee's wedding. She didn't have the heart to ask right now. Not after just hearing the news yesterday and not having the time to process it.

Fran slid in beside Rylee, leaving the other side open for Autumn, and Cara once she arrived.

"Autumn, what am I supposed to do now?" Rylee asked, tears flooding her eyes before they streamed down her face. The girl was a mess, and Autumn couldn't blame her. "Cayden won't talk to me, and I don't know what to say… or even do. This was supposed to be a happy time for us, but now…"

She tossed her hands up and shook her head while looking to Autumn for answers, but Autumn didn't have any advice to give. This was all new for her. She'd never experienced an upsetting event like theirs while planning a wedding. She was now walking blindly in uncharted territory.

"I feel like I should just call off the wedding," Rylee said, sobbing into overly used napkins clenched in her fists.

"Oh, honey, I wish we could tell ya what to do," Fran said, glancing at Autumn with a sympathetic frown. Autumn felt the same way. If only the answers were simple and would come easily… "Have you thought about possibly movin' the wedding date up?"

Rylee glanced at Autumn and back at Fran. "Have the wedding sooner?"

Fran looked between the girls. "Yeah, I don't see why not," she said, a shrug of her shoulders as she looked back to Autumn, hoping she'd help her out. "Could that be an option, Autumn?"

Rylee's eyes focused on Autumn as she waited for an

answer. Autumn knew anything was possible, but it would be rushed and there was always a chance it could turn out to be a nightmare. But if that's what her client wanted, then she'd do her best and give it her all to make their wedding the most memorable. For them and for Cayden's parents.

The thought brought tears to her eyes. She hated crying, and she refused to do so now.

"Yes," she said, the word coming out in a choke as she grabbed her coffee for a quick drink. "We can arrange it however Cayden and Rylee want it to be arranged."

"And with the circumstances," Fran said, patting Rylee's hand, "I think it'd be a good idea to do whatever you and Cayden feel is best. Just know that you've got the best darn wedding planner in the town of Maple Glen, and the best friends, too."

Fran winked at Autumn while she gave Rylee's hand a gentle squeeze. "I'll leave you two to it because I've got some cleanin' to get done around here. You know what they say," Fran said, sliding out of her seat, "a busy body distracts the mind. And right now, I could use a break from all the thinkin'."

With that, she headed back to the counter, leaving Autumn and Rylee to entertain themselves while waiting on Cara to arrive.

Autumn pulled her phone from her bag and checked the time. She couldn't help but wonder where Cara was.

Where are you? You're missing coffee time.

Setting her phone down, she asked, "Do you want to talk about the options, or should we wait until we know more about Scott?"

Rylee nodded. It wasn't exactly clear as to which question was being answered, but Autumn took it as the latter.

"Okay, then, we'll wait and see what we find out once the guys go to Florida."

Instead of taking the rest of the day off from planning, Autumn stayed at Fran's Coffee and worked through her other clients' information. She couldn't help thinking about Cara and wondering if she was okay. It wasn't like her to miss coffee talks, unless there was an emergency.

Autumn glanced at her phone only to be disappointed when the screen was blank. Not a single notification from anyone—including Cara. Setting her phone down on the table, she considered the possibility that Cara went with the rest of her siblings to Florida without telling her. If that was the case, she would at least know she was okay...

She still couldn't silence the nagging voice inside of her that told her to check on Cara. She tried telling herself that Vince would be watching over her, making sure she was okay, but that wasn't enough to make the pestering thoughts go away.

"Fran?" she called out as she slid out of the booth. She'd been there most of the morning with no response from Cara. She needed to make sure her best friend and business partner was okay. The only problem... she didn't have a vehicle. She'd been meaning to buy one, but she hadn't felt the need to until now. She had been walking everywhere she'd needed to go, but now she needed what she didn't have—a car.

"Yes, dear?" Fran asked, moseying her way over to the booth.

"Can I borrow your car?"

Fran responded with a half laugh at first, but quickly said,

"As long as you promise not to run off and leave Maple Glen behind."

"I need to go check on Cara," she said Before she could say another word, Fran pulled her keys from the pocket of her jeans and handed them to her with a look of understanding on her face. "Thank you."

"Do you know the way? Have you been there before?"

She remembered the road Cara had turned on, taking them onto a gravel road that had led them straight to the cabin belonging to Vince and Cara. "Yes, thank you," she said, leaving her pile of notebooks on the table as she headed for the door. "I'll be back."

"Okay, dear," Fran said, a look of concern etched on her face. "Be careful."

"Always am."

She guided the car along the gravel road she'd recalled from her memory. Maple Glen had several gravel roads leading to and from town, but this one was different. It was right off the main road coming into town, and as long as a person headed in the right direction, they wouldn't miss it.

Pulling Fran's vehicle into the driveway, she parked as close to the door as she possibly could. She had sent a message to Charlie, who had responded back no sooner than she had hit send, telling her that they were heading to Florida. They were sitting in the airport as they spoke, and Cara wasn't with them.

She didn't know Vince's number, other than 911, but she wasn't going to call the emergency line unless…

Shaking the thought from her head, she climbed out of her car and headed to the front door. She needed to make sure Cara was okay. It wasn't like her to go without answering her messages and phone calls.

Banging the bottom of her fist against the heavy, wooden

door, Autumn waited a minute before calling out for Cara. She banged on the door once more, but when it didn't open, she kicked into high gear—fight or flight. Adrenaline coursed through her, and thinking the worst, she tried the door. Of course, it was locked.

Circling the cabin, she peered into the windows that were low enough to the ground and on the deck to see in. There was no sign of anyone inside. The place was dead silent.

Her mind raced with options. She could kick in the door... *yeah, right.* Call 911... but what if Cara was just upstairs sleeping? Vince was more than likely patrolling since his SUV wasn't in the driveway, and Mace was surely on duty with him. She didn't know the non-emergency phone number, either. That left her with only one option... break a window and climb inside.

Searching the ground next to her feet for a rock large enough to do the job, her eyes focused on one a few feet from the back porch. She ran down the steps and grabbed the rock, balancing it in her hand as she made her way back to the window.

Taking a deep breath, she released it slowly while winding her arm back, and just as she went to throw the rock, someone called out, "Hey!"

"Cara?" she tossed the rock over the railing and ran to greet Cara with wide-open arms. "Oh my gosh, I thought something happened to you."

"I'm fine," Cara said with a chuckle as she stepped back, allowing Autumn to see that she was, in fact, okay. She was wearing a jogging suit and a headband, but other than that, she was fine.

"Are you sick? Why are you wearing that?" Autumn shook her head and held up a hand. "Wait, don't answer that.

Answer this one instead. Why aren't you headed to Florida with your family right now?"

Cara glanced down at her stomach, placed a hand on it, and looked back at Autumn. "We felt it was best I stay here. My family will let me know as soon as they know something," she said, tears welling in her eyes as she looked at Autumn. Autumn couldn't piece things together fast enough as Cara said, "And flying isn't the best thing to be doing when you're in the first trimester."

"But jogging is?" Autumn's question left her mouth before her brain had a chance to connect the dots. Cara laughed, wiping the sweat from her brow with a towel. "Wait," Autumn said, shaking her head, "did you say *first trimester*? Are you—"

"Yes, Autumn," Cara said, laughing as she grabbed hold of Autumn's hand. "We're pregnant. I mean… Vince and I are, but yeah."

Autumn couldn't help but pull Cara into her arms and squeeze her in a bear hug. This was amazing news. On-top-of-the-world news! How incredible it was for her best friend to be expecting. "Oh my gosh! I can't believe it!" Autumn said, still in shock but processing it just the same. "When did you… how did you… why didn't you tell me?"

Cara raised her hands in defense. "One thing at a time, please. Let's go sit down," Cara said, leading the way to the back porch Autumn had jumped off of only minutes ago. "And I was going to tell you, but I wanted to make sure we cleared the first trimester."

Autumn sat down next to the wooden table separating her from Cara. She glanced at her friend's belly, unable to see any noticeable changes. "How far along are you?"

Cara tipped her head back, resting it on the top of the wooden chair, obviously thinking or counting the days or weeks… or months… "Just past eight weeks. Vince and I were able to hear the heartbeat at the last appointment with the doctor."

Cara's face was glowing as she smiled at Autumn. Autumn felt overjoyed for her best friend and Vince. It was an exciting time for them. "Care Bear, you're having a baby," Autumn said, tears stinging her eyes as she silently thought of how much she wanted a baby of her own. How they'd talked for hours on end when they lived in the city, about how much they wanted the career, but a family full of babies was on their radar as well. It was finally happening. At least for one of them. "I'm so happy for you. I don't know what else to say."

Cara smiled as she leaned forward in her chair. "I promise that I was going to tell you, Autumn. It's just… I didn't want to jinx it, ya know? I was afraid if too many people found out—"

"Care, it's okay. I understand," Autumn assured her, reaching out and taking hold of her hand before giving it a gentle squeeze. "I'm so happy for you. What does Vince think?"

Cara's eyes lit up as she laughed. "Oh boy, he's… I've never seen a man so emotionally invested, and that's an understatement," Cara said, laughing along with Autumn. Autumn couldn't see Vince being emotional, but then again, it was his baby they were talking about. Anything was possible when it came to the news of a little one. "He's already talking about fixing up one of the spare rooms with the sky light for the nursery. And," Cara said, holding up a finger, "not to mention how much he's been talking about names and what he's going to do if it's a boy, or a girl…"

Cara's voice trailed off as she stared off in the distance

before looking back at Autumn. "This is it, isn't it? This is the life I've always wanted, huh?"

Autumn nodded, again the tears streaming down her cheeks, but she did nothing to stop them. "And you've got it. Care, you've got what you've always wanted."

Cara's tear-streaked cheeks matched her friends, and before she knew it, they were both blubbering messes of tears and snot.

"But I'm worried, Autumn," Cara said, using her sweat-filled towel on her face.

"Why? Everything's going to be okay," Autumn assured her, certain her best friend had nothing to fear.

Cara shook her head. "It's not, though. My dad," Cara said, struggling to clear her throat of the emotion threatening to choke her as sobs wracked through her.

"Oh, Care," Autumn said, sliding out of her chair and kneeling at Cara's side. She wrapped her arms around her best friend and pulled her close, wanting her to feel secure and not alone. Autumn would always be there for Cara, no matter what. And even though Cara's father was diagnosed with the meanest and toughest stage of cancer, Autumn knew in her heart that everything was going to be okay. "I'm so sorry. I—"

"He won't be able to see his firstborn grandchild," Cara cried out, hanging on tightly to Autumn. "He won't be able to watch his grandchild—grandchildren—grow up... he won't—"

"Hey," Autumn whispered, rubbing Cara's back and attempting to soothe the pain. "Miracles happen everyday. I know it's hard to believe, but your father's a troublemaker, and I highly doubt he's going to let cancer win the fight."

Cara sat up, leaning back into her chair as she swiped angrily at her fallen tears. "And Cayden's wedding? He's not going to see his own son get married. Everything's a mess. Cayden wants to move the wedding up, and we're not sure that's a good idea. I know that sounds selfish, but it's what's best for dad, ya know?"

"We'll take it one day at a time, Care," Autumn said, knowing it wasn't what Cara wanted to hear.

"I can't lose him, Autumn. I can't lose my dad."

Autumn realized there was nothing she could say to Cara. So instead, she wrapped her arms around her best friend and cradled her as she poured her heart out and set her worries free. Autumn wanted nothing more than to take away the pain the Mitchells were facing, but she also knew from her own experience there wasn't anything anyone could do to make things better. Instead, she would promise to be there, by Cara's and Charlie's side, until they were able to stand on their own without her support.

CHAPTER EIGHTEEN

The plane landed in Florida bright and early, allowing his brothers and sisters plenty of time to grab breakfast and come up with a plan of action. Knowing their mother would be on the edge of a nervous breakdown, they found it necessary to arrive sooner rather than later.

The only problem—he wasn't ready to see his father. He'd seen the commercials with people battling cancer, and it wasn't pretty. There weren't a lot of things that scared him, but that was one thing he wouldn't deny being afraid of—losing his father and seeing his health fade due to an invisible monster overtaking his body.

Tears stung his eyes as he stared straight ahead. He grabbed his luggage—a single suitcase—from the baggage claim and waited patiently for his siblings to gather their things before meeting him at the other end of the line.

"Do you think Mom will even allow us to help out?" Cassie asked, double checking she had everything. "I don't see that happening so easily, do you?"

Charlie shrugged. "There's only one way to find out, and we're doin' it."

His tone was a bit harsh, but he was tired and hungry. He was angry and confused. His father was a good man. A man who never questioned his faith for one second while raising seven kids and facing tough times in not only their family, but their business, too. What did a man have to do to deserve such a degrading diagnosis that would soon take his life? It wasn't fair. None of this was fair.

Knowing their father's health was declining, knowing their mother was on pins and needles trying to take care of everything, and lastly, having to be prepared for the worst while hoping for the best.

"Hey, bro," Carter called out, dragging his luggage behind him, "what's the plan?"

Charlie turned to face his younger brother. Carter was the second youngest of the boys, leaving a ten-year difference between the two of them, but that didn't change the way Charlie interacted with him. Age was just a number. Since all of his siblings were younger than him, he had been their go-to for help, their role model, and someone they took advice from in times like now.

"I have no idea, bud," Charlie said, rubbing a hand over the scruff on his chin. "I guess we wait and see what the others want to do."

Carter grunted beside him, making it obvious he didn't want to wait for the others. Of them all, Carter was the least patient and most impulsive. He was headstrong and determined. He was known for setting his mind on something and not stopping until whatever it involved was finished. An example of Carter's persistence was the day he mentioned he was completing college and becoming a mechanic. He stated he would have his own shop and he'd be the only mechanic in Maple Glen. He'd been focused on making it happen, and no sooner than he set out to accomplish it, he proved to the whole family that he wasn't joking around.

"I know it's hard to sit around and wait, but we have to think of somethin' before we ambush our parents. Besides that, Catie had a last minute thing come up at the bed and breakfast that she needed to figure out. We should wait for her to arrive," Charlie explained, motioning for Carter to follow him to a section of chairs. They could sit and talk for a few minutes while they waited for the other five to get their things. "But you know how Mom is. She's as stubborn as we are, and there's no way she's goin' to allow us to come waltzin' in like we own the place. She isn't goin' to take orders from anyone. You know that as well as any of us, right?"

Carter folded his arms over his chest after taking a seat across from Charlie. The two of them, although ten years apart, resembled each other in other ways. Carter was young and impatient with a smug grin and a chip on his shoulder. The same way Charlie had been once upon a time, or at least, until he opened the bar. Now there was no reason to act tough and invincible. Charlie knew better, and he also knew it would take Carter a few more years of living to realize it, too.

"Anyway, I think Clay and I are goin' to try and talk Mom into bringin' Dad back to Maple Glen," Charlie explained, keeping his voice low as he leaned forward, his elbows on his knees as he looked at Carter. Carter's brow furrowed as he unfolded his arms and leaned forward, matching his brother's body position. Charlie held up a hand to keep Carter silent for a minute. "Before you say anything, just know that it's not up to us… It's up to Mom and whether she feels it's the right thing to do."

"Hey, what's up?" Clayton slid into a nearby chair, interrupting Charlie's conversation with Carter. Charlie waited for

Carter to acknowledge what he'd said before turning his attention to Clayton. "What'd I miss?"

Charlie shook his head. "We were just talkin', is all. Have you heard anythin' from Mom?"

Clayton pulled his phone from his pocket and shook his head. "My phone's been silent since we left Maple Glen."

"That's unusual for you," Charlie teased, nudging his brother with an elbow. "Must be because you brought Emmalee along, huh?"

"What about me?" Emmalee asked, sitting sideways on Clayton's lap and wrapping an arm around him. She looked down at Clayton and smiled before kissing him, and in that moment, Charlie was missing Autumn. He wanted a love like his brothers had found. Something down to earth and simple, not overwhelming and dramatic. He'd had enough drama in the last relationship he'd been involved in to last him a lifetime. It was nothing but complete nonsense.

"So, what's the plan? We need to figure out what's goin' on with Mom and Dad so I can get back to town and figure out what to do about my wedding," Cayden said, dropping his luggage next to an empty chair before plopping down onto it. "Sittin' here isn't gettin' us any further than if we would've just stayed home."

Everyone stopped what they were saying and turned to Cayden, who was now scrolling through his phone, unphased and in his own world. Charlie looked at Clayton, wondering what the heck had gotten into this kid—literally. Cayden was the baby of the family, and right now, it was obvious. How in the world he'd landed a fiancée was beyond Charlie's imagination.

"How about you care for someone other than yourself for once," Cassie said, taking the bait and tearing it to pieces before spitting it out. Charlie smirked. There was the Cassie he knew. She'd been biting her tongue and holding back like the rest of them the whole way to Florida. Charlie had known it would only take a few more jabs from Cayden to get the bear to attack. Not that Cassie was a bear or anything, because she wasn't. She was the sweetest of the sisters and never caused an ounce of trouble. But, she stood up for what she felt was right, and the love she had for their parents ran deeper than the blood inside their veins. "Just shut up about your wedding. You and Rylee can figure it out, I'm sure. That's who you've been textin', right?"

Her eyes were fire, and Charlie leaned back in his chair to avoid being hit in the crossfire.

"For one, I do care about others and not just about myself," Cayden said, setting his phone down in front of him as he returned Cassie's steely glare. "And for two, my wedding is less than a month away, which we still haven't sent out the invites for, and I'm sure there's a laundry list of other things needing to be done that hasn't been started yet. So, yes, Rylee and I are workin' on the details, but I need to get crap figured out sooner rather than later."

Cassie rolled her eyes, and instead of having the last word, Charlie noticed she changed the subject. "Anyone know of a place to grab a quick bite to eat? That will give us some time so we can discuss everything before we get there."

Charlie didn't care where they ended up for breakfast. He would eat whatever and wherever they decided on. He was more worried about his mother's reaction and how she was going to handle the six of them showing up at her door. He didn't want her to think they were charging in and taking over. It wasn't going to be like that at all. Or at least, he sure didn't want it to be.

He wanted his mother to know that she had their support, and if it would help make things better, even a smidge, she could always move back to Maple Glen with their father for the time being.

For the time being. The thought made him sick to his stomach. What would she do once their father decided he was tired of fighting? Would she stay in Maple Glen, or would she move back to Florida?

His phone vibrated inside the pocket of his flannel. Unbuttoning the pocket, he dug it out and opened the message glaring back at him. He hoped it was Cara, telling them she was okay. News had quickly traveled among them once they'd learned of her missing the morning coffee talk with the others. It wasn't like Cara to go without coffee, or conversations with friends. Not to mention work. Autumn had seemed pretty rattled about not hearing from Cara this morning.

She was always worried about everyone else. One of the reasons he fell so hard in love with her. Sure, she was a bit too dedicated to her career, but at the end of the day, she was right there beside him, ready to take on the world with him.

Glancing back at the message on his phone, he smiled.

Found Cara. I think she must be sick because she was out for a morning jog?

His fingers quickly swiped across the screen as he replied back to her.

Get her to the doctor asap. Something is definitely wrong with her.

He chuckled before showing Clayton and Emmalee the message. "Cara's been found," Charlie said, making sure everyone heard him. "I guess she would rather jog than drink coffee now?"

Clayton shook his head and Emmalee shifted on his lap. "I'm just glad that Autumn found her. She was really worried about her."

Another message lit up his phone, so Charlie pulled it out of view from the others. He didn't care if they saw the texts, but he needed to read them first just in case...

I miss you and hope you're doing okay. I'll see you when you get back home.

He wasn't doing okay, but he wasn't going to tell her that. He was bound and determined to find the strength to face whatever stood in their way. He had to be strong, not only for his brothers and sisters, but for his mother, too.

I miss you too. I'll be home soon

Shoving his phone into his pocket, he stood from his chair and said, "Let's get somethin' to eat and then go see our parents."

CHAPTER NINETEEN

"Cara should be comin' any minute," Fran said, sliding into the booth across from Autumn and setting a coffee down in front of her. "What'd she say her reason was for not comin' here yesterday?"

Autumn put her pen down and grabbed the coffee. "Thank you," she said before lifting the cup to her lips and taking a drink. She hadn't mentioned Cara's *special situation* to Fran yesterday afternoon when she brought her car back. She would leave that moment for Cara. "She was out for a morning jog."

Fran nearly spit her coffee out, causing Autumn to quickly pull her planner out of the way. "She what?"

Autumn nodded with a chuckle. She had been just as surprised, if not more, when she'd seen Cara sweating and wearing workout clothes. But she hadn't been as surprised by that as she'd been with the news of Cara's pregnancy. She was over the top with joy about it and couldn't wait to start planning the baby shower.

"Cara doesn't jog," Fran said matter-of-factly, scrunching her nose as she asked. "Since when?"

Autumn shrugged. She didn't know Cara even liked working out. They'd made jokes about working out from time to time while shoving their mouths full of doughnuts.

"That's strange," Fran said, stirring a packet of sugar into her coffee. "I wonder why she's on this new fitness kick. I bet it's 'cause of the weddin'. It's not like she has much to lose. I don't see why she's so concerned."

Autumn bit her tongue. It was hard to keep a secret, but it would be more difficult to apologize to Cara for ruining the surprise.

Autumn thought about the timing of it all... The Mitchell family was facing devastating news regarding Scott while Cara was holding back the overwhelmingly joyful news of expecting a little one.

"Hey, did I miss anything?" Rylee asked, sliding in next to Fran. "I'm sorry I'm late, but Cayden called and told me they're getting ready to head over to Scott and Linda's."

Fran frowned and Autumn nodded. She knew it wasn't going to be easy for the family, so she said a silent prayer and hoped for the best.

"Anyway," Rylee said, fanning her face to avoid the tears welling in her eyes. "I guess we're going to move the wedding up a couple of weeks."

Autumn's eyes widened as she glanced down at the calendar in front of her. Everything was lined up for the original date, but now, looking at the daunting list of items still open and waiting to be checked off...

"Is that going to be possible?" Rylee asked, looking straight at her as Autumn skimmed through the notes she'd scribbled along the edges of the planner. "Cayden said the only other option—"

"It should be fine," Autumn said, cutting Rylee off. There wasn't another option. She would make it work for the

Mitchell family. Scott deserved to see his son get married, and until they knew more than what they did now, time was ticking and Autumn wasn't going to take chances. "I can call the bakery and reschedule with her, and I'll call the preacher and let him know, too. The other things on the list, as long as you've said yes to your dress, are easy to move the date on."

Rylee smiled. "You're the best. I told Cayden we wouldn't have anything to worry about. I told him that you and Cara make a great team."

Autumn smiled, shocked by Rylee's feedback. Not that Autumn thought things were going so horribly that it'd reflect on her ability to plan a successful wedding, but a person could never quite be sure... Especially since things started out a little rough with this one.

"Okay, so we're now looking at the last Saturday in September for your wedding, correct?" Autumn asked, flipping her planner around to show Rylee the calendar. Rylee nodded with a smile. "Okay, then, I'll get started with making some phone calls," Autumn said, pulling her phone out of her bag and sliding out of the booth. She grabbed her phone book, aka wedding planning bible, and headed for a vacant booth several feet behind their current one.

Before dialing the first number on her list, she sent a quick text to Cara. She wanted to give her a heads up, hoping she'd be arriving shortly.

Cayden and Rylee moved the wedding date up. SOS

Before she was able to tap the bakery's contact info, a message buzzed in.

I'll be there soon. I have to shower.

Autumn shook her head, wondering what had gotten into her best friend—aside from the baby. **Jogging again?**

Yes. It's a good feeling. I think they call it a runner's high or something like that?

She chuckled, knowing that's exactly what it was called, but she wasn't ever going to find out for herself.

I'll take your word for it. I won't be jogging anytime soon unless my life depends on it.

She hit send and waited to see if more messages would come through before dialing the bakery's number.

"Hello, this is Bree's Bakery. I'm unable to come to the phone right now. If you'll leave your name and phone number, I'll call you back as soon as I can."

The beep lasted a second, prompting Autumn to begin talking. "Hi, this is Autumn Martin. I called a few weeks ago about needing a cake for the Mitchell wedding in the middle of October. There's been a change of plans, and we're needing that cake sooner than we had originally planned. Please call me back as soon as you get this and let me know if that's possible. Thank you."

Ending the call, she put the phone down on the table in front of her. She had an uneasy feeling in her gut. If there was one thing she'd learned over the years of planning, it was to listen to her gut. Right now, it was telling her something wasn't right, but she couldn't put a finger on what it was, exactly.

"Hey, there you are," Cara said, stalling on her way by Autumn's booth. She combed her fingers through wet hair as she slid in across from Autumn. "I tried to get here as soon as I could. Clayton called me on my way here."

Autumn saw the frown on Cara's face the split second before she tried to hide it. "I just keep thinking that I should be there with them. I should've boarded the plane the second they did, and I'd be there with them to see Dad."

"Care, I'm sure they understand," Autumn said, trying to assure her best friend that family—especially hers—understands. "Especially in your condition," Autumn said, motioning to Cara's stomach hidden by the table. "I'm sure they're going to be back in no time, and if I know them, which I think I know them well enough, they'll be bringing your parents back with them. Or at least that's what Charlie says, anyway."

"I haven't told them about the baby yet," Cara said, folding her hands in front of her and twiddling her thumbs nervously. She shook her head and looked at Autumn as she took her hands off the table. "Okay, I need distractions. These pregnancy hormones are no joke," Cara said, fanning her face and wiping tears away from her eyes.

"Okay," Autumn said, flipping her planner open and grabbing a pen, she motioned for Cara to take a look. "Help me figure out what to do next for your brother's wedding."

"Sure thing," Cara said, glancing over her shoulder then back at Autumn, "but first, can I grab a cup of coffee and somethin' to eat?"

Autumn nodded and grabbed her planner, turning it around to face her. She would look over the rest of her notes to double check she hadn't missed anything the first time through. Two weeks would come quickly, and she could only hope and pray that everything would go smoothly as they transitioned through the date change. She wanted nothing but the best for Cayden and Rylee.

A few hours later, and she felt like the wedding was back on track. Tuxes were rented—the guys having been fitted last month according to Rylee helped matters. Bridesmaid dresses were fitted, but the colors were still up in the air. Rylee promised to have the colors picked by the end of the week.

"That just leaves invitations and the cake," Autumn said, closing her planner and flipping open her notebook. Rylee had given her a list of addresses, for both sides of the family, last week. Autumn had folded the paper and tucked it into the pocket of her notebook. Flipping to the middle of the book, an empty pocket stared back at her. "No... no... no..."

Cara and Rylee, who had been busy chatting amongst themselves, stopped and stared at Autumn. Autumn shuffled through the notebook, a mad attempt to find the list of addresses. It had to be in there somewhere. It hadn't been *that* long since she last looked at it.

"What's wrong?" Rylee asked, but Autumn ignored her. Rylee looked to Cara and back at Autumn. "Is it in there? Please tell me you didn't lose it."

"I didn't," Autumn said, keeping her words short as she continued on with her search. It had to be in the notebook. She hadn't touched it since Rylee had given it to her. She may have pulled it out to see how many names were on it, but that was for just a minute and she slid it right back into its place. "It's gotta be in here somewhere."

Rylee placed her face in her hands and let out a loud sob, causing Fran to rush over to their booth. "What's wrong, dear?" Fran asked, looking to the others for answers, but everyone stayed quiet as Autumn ripped through her notebook. "Uh oh... don't tell me—"

"I'll find it," Autumn promised, flipping through each individual page of the book. "It's in here somewhere. It has to be. A piece of paper can't grow feet and walk away."

Fran kept silent for a minute while she witnessed Autumn's catastrophe. Autumn's mind raced, thinking of the last place she'd put the list. She was more than certain she hadn't misplaced it.

"You have to find it," Rylee said, irritation in her voice. "It took me hours to come up with everyone's address, and that's the only copy."

Autumn sighed, unwilling to give up on the search, but

she did want to bang her head on the table. *So much for things going smoothly.*

"I'm sure Autumn has it somewhere in that pile of hers," Fran said, offering a bit of assurance when Autumn needed it the most. "I'm sure she'll find it before the day's through. Is there anythin' I can get for you, girls?"

Autumn glanced up at Fran, allowing her eyes to say what she couldn't. Pleading for sanity while she silently prayed the rest of the day would get better. "A big cup of another start to the day would be great."

Fran offered a sympathetic smile. "I don't have that, but give me a minute and I'll be right back with somethin' better."

"Thank you," Autumn said, watching Fran walk away with a smile on her face. She couldn't help feeling like she was in the wrong business. Making coffee and offering cups full of happiness to customers seemed to be the job to have. Turning her attention back to her stuff, she pulled her bag onto her lap and began digging through the contents. She chastised herself for not keeping it clean and organized—especially now.

"Maybe you left it at home?" Cara said, offering a subtle smile. "I'm sure it's sitting on the table or maybe on the couch?"

Autumn knew Cara was wrong. There was no way the list could be anywhere but in her bag or inside the folder where she'd last put it. She sighed as she pulled out the last of the junk from her bag. "What else can go wrong?"

Rylee gasped and shook her head. "You should *never* ask that."

Autumn rolled her eyes and offered a half laugh. Of course, someone would be superstitious enough to believe in all of that mumbo jumbo.

Just as she was about to toss her bag to the side, a tattered piece of paper caught her eye. Reaching in, she grabbed a hold of it and brought it out into the sunlight filtering through the window. "Aha! I told you guys that I had it here somewhere!"

Rylee breathed a sigh of relief while Cara patted Autumn on the back. "Well done. Now, let's get started on these invites."

Autumn nodded and offered Rylee a reassuring smile. "Yes, let's do this."

They'd have them filled out and mailed off by the end of the day today—no *ifs*, *ands*, or *buts* about it.

CHAPTER TWENTY

After Catie's late arrival, they were finally able to make their way to their parent's house. Given the extra day, Charlie still found himself unprepared for how frail his father would be. If Charlie had been anyone other than who he was, he wouldn't have recognized the man sitting in front of him.

A pale complexion stared back at him as each of his siblings took a seat in the living room. They gathered around their father, who was sitting slumped to the side of his favorite recliner with sunken eye sockets displaying his prominent cheekbones.

"Hey, Dad," Charlie said, sitting closest to his father's chair. An oxygen tank leaned next to the stand separating the couch from his father's chair. A narrow tube leading to his father's nose assisted his father's breathing the best it could given the circumstances.

"Hey, Son," Scott said, his voice rough like sandpaper. "What're y'all doin' here? Don't ya have work to do?"

Charlie looked down at his folded hands and back at his father, offering a smirk. Of course, his father would be more concerned about their businesses than himself. "We came to see you, Dad."

Scott's eyes found his, and in that split second, Charlie was able to see his father. *Eyes are the window to the soul, or so they say...*

Charlie cleared his throat and angrily swiped a stray tear from his cheek. It wasn't supposed to be like this. His father had just retired. He still had plenty of life left to live and enjoy while seeing his kids marry and have kids of their own.

"I'm fine," Scott said, shooing away any argument saying differently. "I don't know what the big fuss is. A little cancer never hurt nobody. Besides, you can't get rid of me that easily."

To his left, Charlie heard his sisters choke back a sob as they hugged each other tightly. He wanted to believe his father. He'd give anything to believe he was fine and it was nothing more than a flu bug making him sick. But it wasn't.

"Your father has been fightin' the doctor since day one," Linda said, walking into the living room with a tray of drinks —mostly iced sweet tea and water. She handed them out accordingly, making sure no one went without. Charlie grabbed a glass and said thanks before taking a long drink. The Florida heat was nothing unlike the heat they'd faced in the midwest. "Your dad's convinced he'll live forever, no matter what he's got."

Charlie watched his father's reaction to his mother's words. With a slight eye roll and a shake of the head, it was obvious the man was in denial. "I'm fine, Linda," he said, plucking the pronged tube from his nostrils. "I don't even need this, but *they* insist I wear it. No matter how many times I say I'm fine without it."

"We've gone over this, Scott," Charlie's mother said, a flustered expression crossing her face. Charlie could tell his mother was at her wits' end with everything going on around them. "You need the oxygen to help you breathe," she said as she slapped his hand away from the tubing and replaced each prong inside the respective nostrils. "Now leave it well enough alone."

His father chuckled, throwing himself into a coughing fit that left Charlie and his siblings on the edge of their seats as their mother rubbed his back and assured them it was okay.

"Deep breaths," Linda coached, softly running a hand up and down Scott's back. "There ya go. Nice and easy."

Charlie glanced at his brothers and sisters, who like him, were taken aback by the fear and reality of the situation. No one had expected it to be as bad as it was. Sure, they'd all heard cancer, but the severity hadn't hit them until now. A slap in the face with a dire wake-up call prompted them into action.

"Mom..." Cassie said, standing from her seat and walking toward her mother, "Dad, come back to Maple Glen with us. Let us help take care of things."

The emotion caused a tremble in Cassie's voice and a quiver in her bottom lip as she held back the tears. "You can always stay at any of our places, or heck," Catie said, standing next to Cassie, "you can enjoy the hospitality of my B and B if ya'd like. Granted, I'm still in the process of fixin' it up, but I'm sure I can make up a room just for you guys."

Their mother shook her head, fighting back tears as she said, "We're fine here where we are. We've got the best oncologist in the state of Florida for your father, and we wouldn't have that back home."

Charlie knew they couldn't disagree with that. Their mother had a point. Their father deserved the best care he could get, and Maple Glen couldn't offer much in comparison.

"We're movin' my weddin' up," Cayden said, standing on the other side of Clayton. Linda's eyes widened, allowing the tears that had once been barricaded to break free. "It's in two weeks, and we want you guys there."

"Two weeks?" Linda asked, looking at Cayden like he'd lost his mind. The underlying reason for the change of date didn't need to be explained. Their mother knew why, and by the look in her eyes, she wasn't going to say no. "Well, alright then," she said, lightly patting Scott on the back. "We better get movin'. I've got a few things needin' taken care of, but I can have us ready to go by…"

She turned toward a calendar hanging across the room. "What's today? Ah, nevermind, I see it. When are y'all headin' back?"

Charlie looked to his sisters and brothers who shrugged in response. They hadn't expected their mother to agree so quickly to come back home. Granted, it took a wedding, but still…

"As soon as we can," Cayden said, shuffling his stance as he waited impatiently for a decision to be made. "There's still a few things we need to set up and take care of. Rylee and Autumn are needin' help with a few things, too. Cara's been doin' what she can to help, but lately she's been duckin' out."

Charlie raised a brow in Cayden's direction. *Ducking out? What the heck for?* Cayden shrugged, and that answered that. Charlie would ask Autumn about it later when he got back to the hotel room. If Cara wasn't helping Autumn, and the wedding was closer now than before, that meant the stress was put on Autumn…

"Okay, then," Linda said, breaking Charlie's thoughts, "book the next flight out. I'll call and make arrangements with the doctor and make sure everything in your father's medical file gets sent to Dr. Stevens."

"I'll book it now," Clayton said, standing and making his way to the kitchen. Linda watched him walk away and turned back to the others.

"Are you guys hungry?" she asked, "I can whip somethin' up real quick."

It was in their mother's nature to offer comfort food in times like now. They would allow her to cook them something to eat, because it was obvious she needed the distraction. She needed something to do to take her mind off of the reality she was facing.

"Sounds good, Mom," Charlie said, sneaking past her and walking out onto the back porch. He needed a moment to clear his thoughts and the overwhelming threat they all faced in losing their father. He wanted to spend every last minute with the man that he possibly could, and he would, but first, he needed to send a message back home to Autumn. He needed to check to see if she'd heard from Cara lately. It wasn't like his sister to *duck out* of important matters, especially when everything was falling apart.

Plus, it gave him a reason to check on Autumn, too. With everything happening so fast, he couldn't imagine the amount of stress Autumn was left facing alone. Even if it was her job, and even if she was good at what she did, he still felt the need to make sure she was doing okay.

CHAPTER TWENTY-ONE

"There," Autumn said, closing her planner, "everything's done."

She'd taken a day to catch up on her other clients' work along with the Mitchell wedding, and now Rylee and Cayden's wedding was all set. Other than a few hiccups along the way, not to mention moving everything up two weeks, everything else had gone smoothly.

Now, as long as said things stayed in line and together, Autumn didn't foresee any last minute emergencies.

"*Done,* done?" Rylee and Cara asked in unison, each giving the other a puzzled look. "Wow, that went better than I expected."

"Knock on wood," Autumn said, pointing to the table. "Don't jinx us. We still have to get through this week."

The past week had been full of random emotions and late-night phone calls from Charlie. She was more than thankful he'd decided to call her each night he was in Florida, giving her an update on his father's condition and chemo treatments. They'd all thought their parents would have been able to come back home right away, but the oncologist had other thoughts. He'd thought it would be best for Scott to have a week's worth of chemo and radiation before making the trip back.

Autumn wasn't sure what all that entailed, but from what she gathered during the phone calls with Charlie, it wasn't easy. She wanted nothing more than to reach through the phone and wrap her arms around him. She could hear the agony in his voice, his emotions getting the best of him as he cleared his throat often.

Thankfully, the days were flying by and they would be back home soon. And then it would be time for the wedding.

"You're the best," Rylee said, wrapping her arms around Autumn's shoulders, pulling Autumn from her thoughts. "Thank you so much."

Autumn smiled, knowing her job wasn't done just yet. She would still need to follow up with the businesses, decorators, and the caterers and make sure everything was still set in stone for the upcoming weekend. She was hopeful that everything would go as planned, but as a planner, she'd learned over the years to never hold her breath. If a million and one things could go wrong, they would. It was the whole *Murphy's Law* thing.

"Let's just get through this week and get the Mitchells back home before we get too excited," Autumn said, patting Rylee's arm. She didn't want to be a negative Nancy, but she couldn't settle her thoughts until the weekend came and the wedding was over and done. "Is there any other last-minute things you'd like to get done? If so, now's the time to do them."

Rylee nodded as she glanced at her phone. "I could take the day and go see my mom and sisters. They'd love to see me as much as I would love to see them."

Autumn smiled. "Sounds good. If I need anything, I'll give you a call."

Rylee nodded and slid out of the booth, waving goodbye to Cara and Fran who were busy behind the counter preparing coffee and lattes. Even though Fran said she'd hired a part-timer to help with the rushes, Autumn hadn't met him yet. He'd been there a time or two while they were gone, Fran had said, but Autumn and Cara weren't so sure.

"So," Fran said, sliding into the vacant side of the booth and offering a freshly made latte to Autumn. Autumn smiled and gladly accepted it. She loved Fran's lattes as much as the next person. "What's this I hear about the plannin' side of things being done?"

Autumn sipped her drink through the straw and nodded. She put her cup down and said, "I marked off the last thing from my to-do list. Other than a few odd and ends here and there, everything is good to go."

Fran brought her coffee cup to her lips but kept it there without taking a drink. Instead, she focused her eyes on the liquid inside, contemplating her next words before saying, "I guess Scott's doin' a lot better than expected since startin' those treatments?"

Autumn looked for Cara, finding her behind the counter still busying herself with coffee refills and taking orders. Autumn shook her head, knowing how much Cara had enjoyed filling in at the coffee shop during what seemed to be forever ago.

She didn't mean to ignore Fran's statement. She simply didn't know what to say. Talking to Charlie had been difficult, because no matter what, Scott's prognosis was still the same —he had only months to live, and his doctor wasn't sure if the treatments would even touch the cancer spreading like wildfire through his body. The thought saddened Autumn as she thought of the future and what all would be missed once Scott…

Nope. She wasn't going to think that. She'd read several stories online about miraculous recoveries and triumphant wins regarding cancer diagnoses. Scott had a fighting chance, and she wouldn't take that away from him.

"Linda called yesterday afternoon and mentioned it to me," Fran continued on, not caring if Autumn was listening or not. Autumn gave her undivided attention, wanting to engage in conversation with Fran because Scott was, in fact, Fran's brother-in-law. "She thinks they'll be here mid-week. The kids are stayin' out there until Linda and Scott are okayed to come back home."

Autumn nodded. Charlie had told her the same information the other night. He'd wanted to call and make sure she was doing okay, but in all reality, Autumn had told him she was more worried about him and his family than she was herself. The stress she'd gone through for the wedding was nothing in comparison to what the Mitchells were facing.

"I can't wait to see them," Autumn said, scooting over and allowing Cara to slide in next to her.

"I think what you meant to say is that you can't wait to see a certain someone," Fran said with a wink as she reached across the table and nudged Autumn in the arm. Autumn felt the heat creep into her cheeks as she looked down at her drink. "Maybe," she said, "but I'd love to see Linda and Scott, too."

"I know that, dear," Fran said, patting her hand. "I'm sure they're goin' to love seein' us, too."

Autumn's phone buzzed against the table, pulling her away from the conversation. Cara and Fran continued on talking about Scott's treatments while Autumn answered the incoming call from the bakery.

"Autumn?"

"This is she."

Autumn could hear a sense of urgency in the baker's voice, and she quickly said a silent prayer everything was okay.

"I'm so glad you answered," the woman said in a rush. "I hate to cancel your reservation on such short notice, but I've had a family emergency come up, and I'm needed back home for my mom and dad. I'm so sorry."

"Oh, I'm sorry to hear that. I hope everything's going to be alright," Autumn said. "Thank you for letting me know."

"I sure hope so," the woman said. "Thank you for understanding. I'm getting ready to board the plane now. Again, I'm so sorry for canceling at the last minute."

"No worries," Autumn assured her, "take care."

"Thank you."

A click on the other end of the line ended the call, and the reality of what had just occurred hit Autumn in the gut. She was now without a baker... which meant she was now without a cake for the wedding... A wedding that was happening in less than seven days. The same wedding Rylee had thanked her for planning and getting everything put together.

"Oh no," Autumn said, putting her phone down on the table and placing her head in her hands. She couldn't believe her luck. She knew luck had nothing to do with it, but still... she had known something would go awry.

"Uh oh," Cara said, calling attention to the unfortunate news Autumn received. "Not a good call?"

"What's wrong, dear?" Fran asked, pulling Autumn's hands away from her face. The stress of the planning, accompanied with the family's dire news about Scott, and now the cake pushed Autumn past the breaking point. Tears streamed down her cheeks as she looked at Cara then back at Fran. She had no words to explain the overwhelming sense of failure she felt deep inside. To think that everything would have turned out as planned had been a joke, but no one was laughing. Instead, they were watching her and waiting for her to explain what happened. "Who was it that called?"

"The baker," Autumn said, her words not sounding like her own as the stress broke her into a sobbing mess. "She has a family emergency and canceled the cake."

"Oh, well, I'm sure we can find someone to bake a cake for the weddin'," Fran said, glancing from Autumn to Cara. "There's bound to be someone who knows how to bake a cake around here."

Autumn looked at Cara, who shook her head as she, along with Autumn, waited for Fran to say *who* the person was that she had in mind. Because the last time Autumn had checked, there was only one baker in Maple Glen, and they had once made a comment in regards to Bree hiring an assistant just in case. And now...

"It's me, girls," Fran said, pointing confidently to herself. "I'm the *who* that knows how to bake a cake."

"Really? You would do that?" Autumn said, sighing in relief. "I would love you forever if you're sure you want to."

Fran leaned back with a chuckle and said, "Well, I sure hope you'd love me forever regardless of if I make the cake or not."

Autumn smiled. "Of course, I just meant—"

"I know, dear. I have no problem makin' a cake for the weddin'," Fran said, a bright smile on her face. "I might even see if Linda wants to help. I think it'd do her some good to take her mind off things while helping out with her son's weddin' cake."

Autumn nodded, and from the smile on Cara's face, Cara

agreed as well. Maybe Autumn had been wrong about *Murphy's Law*. And maybe, just maybe, the wedding would go without a hitch—no pun intended.

The Mitchell family arrived back home in Maple Glen two days before the wedding, leaving just enough time for everyone to cross the final things off their to-do lists—including baking the cake, which Fran was determined to finish by the night before, confident in her and Linda's baking abilities. There was even a slight mention from someone who had overheard the two of them contemplating opening their own bakery or assisting with Bree's business. It was something the *coffee talk girls* were looking into.

As for right now, Fran was standing in the Deli's kitchen, prepping ingredients for a three-tier wedding cake while Linda gathered the equipment needed.

Autumn sat with Cara, occasionally asking the two sisters if they'd like any help, but giving up on asking after the third time of being told *'We've got this all taken care of.'*

"Okay, then," Autumn said, glancing back at Cara, who offered her a knowing look. "It looks like we're no longer needed here. What should we do?"

"I don't know about you, but I'm thinking we should take the rest of the day off and catch up on *I Love Lucy* reruns while we eat ice cream."

Autumn loved that idea. A girl and her best friend could never go wrong with watching a good show and eating ice cream.

"Sounds perfect," Autumn said, standing from her seat and heading to the counter separating them from the kitchen.

"Hey, ladies, we're heading out. We'll be at my place. So if you need us, just call."

Without so much as a nod and a quick mumble, Fran and Linda continued on with their mission in the kitchen.

Autumn turned back to Cara and asked, "Are you ready?"

"Ready as I'll ever be."

EPILOGUE

"Are you ready? Everyone's seated in the church pews waitin'," Charlie said, knocking on the door of the groom's room in the back of the church.

"I'm ready," Cayden said, pulling the door open and walking out into the hallway. "It's now or never, right?"

"That's right," Charlie said with a smile. His little brother was getting married. At a time when they should be happy and proud, there was also solace and concern for their father, and a nagging thought of how much longer they had to spend with him. "Let's go and find your bride."

Walking down the hall, Cayden stopped and shook his head. "I don't think I can do this."

Charlie stopped walking and turned to face his brother. "What? Now's not the time to—"

"I mean... seeing Dad and knowing he isn't going—"

"Cayden, stop right there," Charlie said, holding up a hand and shaking his head. "Let's take it one day at a time. We've got to take life as it comes. There's no sense in worryin' about what's comin' when there's so much happenin' now. You're gettin' married, bro. Focus on that for now. Everything else is in God's hands."

With a slight nod, Cayden walked forward, arriving at the entrance of the aisle a few minutes later. Charlie offered his brother a hug before leaving him with their mother and finding Autumn in the pews.

It wasn't hard to find her. She was the most beautiful woman in the crowd, and her brown eyes were looking right at him. "Is this seat taken?"

"Only by a handsome bartender I've had the pleasure of meeting and falling in love with," she teased, batting her eyelashes at him. "That wouldn't happen to be you, would it?"

He pulled at the side of his tux and adjusted his tie. "I think that pretty much sums me up," he said, sliding in next to her. "I only have a minute, but I wanted to say thank you for everythin' you've done for me and my family."

She smiled, with tears shining in her eyes, and nodded. "I have no regrets. I really like your family," she said, offering him a teasing grin before saying, "and I like you, too."

"Oh yeah? Just *like*?"

"I don't know," she said, playing with the curls in her hair and wrapping them around her finger. "There might be a little bit of love, too."

It was only a few short days ago that he arrived back in town from Florida with his family in tow. He had checked the mail and found the invitation to the wedding. Finding it odd, because he was in the wedding, he opened it. Of course, it was an invitation he assumed to be like the rest, but it was his reply that would make it different. He needed a date to the wedding, and he couldn't think of anyone he'd rather be with than Autumn Martin.

Along the bottom of the invite, in the section requesting his response, he wrote:

RSVP for Two - Charlie and Autumn

He had given the invitation back to Cara with special instruction—*Autumn's eyes only*—and he timed it perfectly while waiting for her to call.

"I love you, too," he said, pecking her lips with a quick kiss before making his way to the front and standing in his assigned place next to his brothers. He looked out over the crowded pews, his eyes landing on the girl of his dreams, who he couldn't wait to make his wife, and winked with a smile.

Rattling cans attached to the back of his brother's car could be heard for miles as they drove down the road. Honking cars led the way to Charlie's Bar and Grill. Charlie smiled at Autumn, who was now sitting next to him in his truck, eager to see the decorations at the bar.

He had to give her props for arranging the decorations and lining everything up. His bar might have been manly last week, but today, he knew that would not be the case. He thought back to the day he'd teased and had taken it a bit too far. The day she got angry and he almost lost her for good.

"What are you thinking about?" she asked, smiling back at him wearing a beautiful, flower-patterned sundress and curls in her long, dark hair. There was something to be said about a woman like Autumn. She was stubborn and fierce when she had something in mind, but she sure knew how to steal a man's heart, too. "You're wearing that Cheshire grin and looking at me like I'm a piece of meat. Cut it out."

She playfully smacked his arm and said, "I can't wait for

you to see the frillies. Your bar is completely covered in flowers and girly decorations."

He nodded and kept his eyes on the road. He wouldn't admit to what he'd been thinking, and he also wouldn't admit to being the slightest bit excited to see what the inside of his bar looked like. It was, in fact, only for a day. He could deal with the girly stuff for that long.

Following the cars, he pulled into the parking lot next to his bar and shifted into park. Killing the engine, he looked over at her and asked, "Are you ready?"

She smiled back at him and pulled the handle, opening the door before climbing out. "Ready as I'll ever be," she said, slamming the door and meeting him at the hood of his truck. She reached out for his hand, and he gladly accepted. "But please do me a favor?"

"Anythin' for you," he said, and he meant it. He would do whatever she said without the least bit of hesitation.

"Don't do anything crazy," she said, pointing a warning finger at him before continuing their walk toward the entrance of his bar.

"Crazy? Define crazy," he teased, pulling her close and planting a kiss on the top of her shaking head. He was crazy about her, that was a definite, but he didn't plan on proposing or acting a fool just yet. That would come at a later date.

Besides, from the looks of it, Clayton was down on his knee and proposing to Emmalee when they walked inside. A crowd gathered round and cheers erupted with a thunderous clap. Cayden shook his head, and before they knew it, one of the coffee girls was calling out *'I knew it! I win!'*

He looked to Autumn for an explanation on what that was all about, but she shook her head and said, "We might have taken bets on when Clayton would propose to Emmalee."

He smiled, wondering if they'd do the same when it came

time for him to propose to Autumn. He couldn't wait to find out.

Glancing around, he was impressed with what he saw. Aside from the promised frilly decorations, he could deal with the lighting and centerpieces on the tables. It no longer looked like *his* bar, and that was okay. It meant that Autumn had done her job well in hiring a decorator and arranging things just right.

"You're pretty good at this wedding stuff, ya know?"

"I know," she said with a wide grin on her face.

After the father-daughter, mother-son, and the bride and groom's dances were over, he looked at Autumn, who was now sitting beside him at the counter sipping a well-deserved mixed drink. Her eyes shined with tears as she watched Rylee and Cayden on the dance floor. He knew in his heart that is what she wanted the most—the happiness and love that she could only find here in Maple Glen. It had taken them awhile to confess to one another what it was they truly wanted. They could both be stubborn and strictly business-minded, but at the end of the day, they both knew it was each other they wanted the most.

One of the songs they'd sung together during their karaoke night played over the speakers, and Jackson pointed in their direction with a smile. Charlie wouldn't pass up the opportunity to dance with Autumn.

He reached for her drink and set it behind them on the counter. When she looked at him like he had lost his mind, confused on what his intentions were, he asked, "May I have this dance with the girl I love with all my heart?"

She smiled and slid off the barstool, allowing him to lead her to the open space in front of them. As the lyrics of "You Had Me From Hello" by Kenny Chesney surrounded them, he pulled her close and inhaled the scent of lilacs in her hair.

In that moment, he made a silent vow to never let her go and to love her forever. The feeling they shared between them was too good to mess up… that much he knew for certain.

"You know this song's right, don't ya?" he asked, pulling her back in order to look into her eyes. She nodded with a smile, and it was then and only then, he said, "You really did have me from hello, but I was just too damn stubborn to admit it."

She smiled once again, pulling him close once again as she wrapped her arms around his waist. She looked up at him and softly whispered, "I know."

A NOTE FROM THE AUTHOR

If you enjoyed reading *RSVP for Two*, please consider leaving a review.

Thank you!

ABOUT THE AUTHOR

Christina Butrum launched her writing career in 2015 with the release of The Fairshore Series.

Writing contemporary fiction, she brings realistic situations with swoon-worthy romance to the pages - allowing her readers to fall in love right along with the characters.

When she isn't busy writing, Christina enjoys spending time with her family. Christina Butrum looks forward to publishing many more books for her readers to enjoy.

www.authorchristinabutrum.com

Sign Up for Christina's Newsletter Here: http://eepurl.com/cEWfGT
Join Christina's Group Here:
https://www.facebook.com/groups/ButrumsBookBabes

- facebook.com/authorcbutrum
- twitter.com/authorcbutrum
- amazon.com/author/christinabutrum
- bookbub.com/profile/christina-butrum

ALSO BY CHRISTINA BUTRUM

FAIRSHORE SERIES

Second Chances

Unexpected Chances

Fair Chances

KATE'S DUET

Kate's Valentine

Kate's Forever

CEDAR VALLEY SERIES

All She Ever Wanted

Everything She Needed

All She Ever Desired

A MAPLE GLEN ROMANCE SERIES

It Takes Two

Coffee for Two

RSVP for Two

Room for Two - *Coming Soon!*

Lesson for Two - *Coming Soon!*

One plus Two - *Coming Soon!*

STANDALONE NOVELS

No Place Like Home - Love in Seattle

Saving Jenna

INTERCONNECTED NOVELLA

Sweet on Love - A Lover's Landing Novella

Made in the USA
Middletown, DE
09 July 2019